Contents....

The Snake Charmer of Sankranti

Chapter 1   *Sankranti Kurup*

Sankranti Kurup was a snake charmer. He had made his living performing with snakes for as long as he could remember. It was rumoured that Kurup had been raised by a cobra. This was untrue. As an infant he had been abandoned by the roadside. Kalainathan the snake charmer had found him and raised him. The boy had grown up amidst Kalainathan's snakes. He slept with them and sharing their milk. He had respect for the snakes but did not fear them. Even the untimely death of his mentor Kalainathan did not change his perception of the creatures.

Kalainathan had tried to goad an irascible cobra into putting up a performance. The snake had responded with a venomous bite. With his mentor's death, he had inherited the brood of snakes. There had been no other claimants for the bounty. To earn his livelihood, he had continued the trade, moving from fair to fair and making his snakes perform.

The Sankranti festival was a good time for Kurup. He was a regular there. The fair would go on for almost a month. Tradesmen from all over the district would come there to display and sell their wares. It was a rural shopping extravaganza. Families would buy their needs for the entire year at the fair ground.

 Kurup had a special corner at the Sankranti. Every year he would settle at the same corner with his snake baskets. As the crowds started coming in, he would choose which snake to call out to perform. All the baskets had the snake's names inscribed on them. Snakes are notoriously hard of hearing, depending on their sense of vibration. The snake charmer's pipe was his method of communication. The snakes could sense the melody of the pipes. If they were in a good mood they would oblige with a performance. Snakes were however finicky creatures. You could push them just a wee bit. Many snake charmers died when they took their charges for granted. Over a period of time, snake charmers became partially immune to snake venom, but a full blown cobra bite could still be fatal.

The snakes were fed small chicken which Kurup bought from the local market. This Sankranti had been good. Hordes of children had flocked to see the great snake charmer. Women had squawked in fear as he wrapped Shika the cobra round his neck. He usually performed with one snake at a time. If there were two of them out at the same time their behaviour would become more unpredictable. Snakes were jealous creatures. He had to distribute his attention equitably. His latest acquisition was Brenda the cobra. He was a magnificent king cobra. The other snakes would move out of the way when Brenda was brought in.

Chapter 2   A Special Visitor

One day, he had a special visitor. A large luxury car drew up at the fair's parking lot. An imposing Englishman, dressed in a lounge suit exited. His weather-beaten face and tanned complexion suggested that he was an outdoors man. His wife was a study in contrasts. She looked pale and delicate. She carried a parasol to protect herself from the morning sun. Their daughter was a mischievous imp. She must have been about eight years old. She wore a frilly dress and white shoes. Her hair was held up in a single bunch by a pink band. She spotted Kurup and his snakes as soon as she got out of the car. "Dada, a snake charmer", she squealed with joy. Before her parents could stop her she had run to Kurup's corner.

Kurup had a family of four seated in front of him. Brenda was dancing for them. His magnificent hood with its deathly spectacles was spread fully. The girl ran around the seated spectators. She tripped over the snake baskets lid and she fell, right on top of the dancing cobra. There was a hushed silence. Brenda coiled himself around the girl's neck and raised his head to strike. He was looking straight at her and she stared back at him with an absurd fearlessness.

There was a scream and a thud. The lady with the parasol had fainted. The rest of them were frozen into immobility.

Kurup knew that any sudden movement or distraction could induce Brenda to attack. Then the girl did something stupid. She brought up her hand to pat Brenda on the hood as though he were a friendly dog. Brenda's head drew back, his forked tongue darting in suspicious anger. The girls hand followed. Brenda flicked his tongue at the hand. He then uncoiled himself from around her neck and slid back into his basket. Kurup closed the basket's lid. A collective gasp went up from the crowd. The girl picked herself up off the floor, dusted herself and ran back to her father who held her in a tight hug.

There was a babble of voices now. Men from nearby shops had come out. Some were pointing their finger at the girl. The lady with the parasol was sitting up now, colour slowly returning to her face. The man was checking his daughter for telltale marks of the snake's fangs. He beckoned Kurup. Kurup walked up to him. "The snake did not bite her"? Kurup shook his head. He handed Kurup a fifty rupee note and escorted the family to the car.

Chapter 3   Katrina

The lady insisted that they go to the mission hospital for a check-up. Collins the young physician there listened to the story. He checked the girl for bite marks. There were none. There were no signs of envenomation. The girl seemed well, but it was better to be careful. He admitted the girl in hospital for overnight observation. The VIP room was opened and a special nurse kept on duty to regularly check the girl for any effects of poison. It was not every-day that the governor's daughter was treated at their hospital. The next morning the girl was well and cheerful. It was decided that she could go home.

Kurup had packed his snakes and returned to his hut. He had been rattled by the morning's events. If Brenda had bitten the governor's daughter, there would have been hell to pay. He took the rest of the day off. The next morning, he opened the baskets. It was feeding time for the snakes. He got a shock when he opened Brenda's basket. It was empty. Brenda had disappeared. Was his snake loose on the fair-grounds somewhere? He ran to the Sankranti to check. There was no sign of Brenda.

The Governor and his family returned to their bungalow. The servants were rapturous to see their little princess safe and sound. The governor had an official commitment later in the day. He had a quick breakfast and left. His wife retired to her room to sleep. The lady had not slept for most of the night. Katrina retired to her room.

An hour later the stillness of the morning was shattered by a loud scream. It was Kaliamma the maid. She had taken Katrina's breakfast up to her room. There, on the bed covers was Katrina, playing with a king cobra. Brenda had lovingly wrapped around the girl's wrist and she was patting him on his spread hood. By the time the other servants and Katrina's mother came running up Brenda was gone. Kaliamma was sitting on the floor outside the girl's room sobbing. Katrina was lying comfortably in bed reading a book of fables.

When Kurup checked his baskets the next day Brenda was back. As the basket had been kept closed at night it was a mystery as to how Brenda had got in. Some snakes have strange magical powers. Quickly he fed his snakes. It was time for the Sankranti.

When the governor came back, he found his wife hysterical. The king cobra had come to visit their daughter. He tried to pacify her. If the snake had wanted to harm her, he could have, many times, by now. Katrina was unconcerned by all this debate. Brenda was her friend. He would come and visit her again.

Chapter 4   Brenda and Katrina

Over a period of time the governor's house got used to Brenda. In the mornings sometimes he would be seen sleeping next to Katrina. He would leave as soon as the household awakened. The Governor vetoed his wife's suggestion that they trap and kill the snake. There was something magical about him and Katrina would have been devastated if he were hurt. Kurup meanwhile got used to Brenda's mysterious disappearances. He had however, no idea as to where he was going.

Years went by. Katrina grew up into a beautiful young woman. She had been educated through a series of private tutors. Katie was especially gifted in music. By the time she was fifteen, she was giving concerts to packed halls in colonial India. Her personal life however was a bit of a mystery. Young English army officers stationed in India would call on the governor and try to woo her. Her stoic disinterest in her suitors was worrying her mother. Her mind is warped by that snake, her mother would say, for Brenda was still a frequent visitor.

The days of British India were almost over. It would soon be time for the Governor and his entourage to return to England. Katrina was now in charge of a school of fusion music which was founded as an experiment. They were working on merging Indian and Western classical music styles. This center had been getting a lot of interest from the international music community. She would need to stay back in India for a while. Reluctantly her parents agreed. Her mother was concerned. It was time for Katrina to find a suitable English boy. The governor however supported her. He had been receiving glowing reports regarding Katrina's work and he was proud of her. She had a right to forge her own destiny.

The governor and his wife returned to respectable retirement in the English countryside. The lady was soon catching up on all the social niceties that they had missed in India. They had a regular stream of visitors and a packed social life. They received regular missives from Katrina. The classical fusion experiment was a great success. She would try and shift her centre to England as soon as possible. There was also a vague mention of an Indian prince whom she was seeing.

Kurup was still a wandering snake charmer. Brenda and the other cobras performed for him all over the state. He had come to accept Brenda's nightly disappearances as an inexplicable magical phenomenon. In the day Brenda would be back in his basket. Sometimes he would appear in his basket only later.

One night when Kurup was sleeping, he was awakened by a rustle in the grass outside his window. He looked outside. There were two cobras cavorting in the grass. One was Brenda. The other was a female cobra of great beauty. Brenda had found a mate. He watched them. They disappeared for a while and then returned again. Brenda reared himself to his full height outside the window. He had in his jaws a snake charmer's pipe of great beauty. He left the pipe, in front of Kurup on the window sill. Kurup did not move. He recognized the pipe for what it was. He had heard of the mythical snake king's pipe from his mentor Kalainath. With this pipe in his hands, there was no snake that would not obey him. Brenda was giving him a parting gift.

Chapter 5   Wedding Bells

The governor and his wife were in their garden when the butler got them the message. Katrina was returning to England. She would be bringing with her the man she wished to marry, the Indian prince. The old couple received them at the airport. The man was tall, sinuous and slender and was strikingly handsome. His manners were perfect and his demeanour charming. He had won over their trust and affection in no time. The news of Katrina's return with the Indian prince whom she would marry spread through the county.

A steady stream of their friends would drop by. They wanted to see and gauge this new addition to their society. They were impressed beyond their wildest expectations. Katrina's Beau was a prince indeed. An engagement ceremony was held, soon to be followed by a glamorous wedding.

Katrina and her husband made a magnificent couple. The young ladies in the congregation tittered nervously and whispered to each other. "Just look at the prince's eyes. They are so cruelly hypnotic.

Miles away at Sankranti, Kurup was entertaining the crowds with his dancing snakes. He had the magic pipe to his lips. Suddenly the music changed. Kurup was not blowing. The pipes however continued to play a melody of their own. The music was unfamiliar and all the snakes had risen in their baskets and were swaying to the rhythm. A Christian priest who had recently come from England suddenly stopped. He beckoned to his family to be still. He asked, "Do you recognize the music the snake charmer is playing?" They shook their heads. "It is the wedding march".

The Immigrant

Chapter 1   Bijumon

Bijumon drove a taxi. It was not one of those black and yellow painted cabs you saw at taxi stands. It was a tourist taxi. If you telephoned Bijumon he would come and pick you up, to take you to another city or to the airport. The taxi had cost him the princely sum of four and a half lakh rupees. Most of this amount had been taken as a loan from a private bank. The government nationalized banks were notoriously tardy at giving vehicle loans. They had their reasons. Vehicle loans were notoriously difficult to recover legally. It was even more difficult if the vehicle got damaged in an accident.

Private bankers had their own modus operandi for recoveries. Biju had had to sign a hundred forms before the money was given to him. This included a sales deed stating that Biju had sold the car to the bank. If the loans were paid back on time, the bankers would be gentlemen. The owners sometimes refused to or were unable to pay the monthly remittance. The bank would then contact a recovery agency. One of the recovery men would hire the cab. In a quiet place, he would tell the driver who he was. The driver would be made to get off the car and the car driven off to a garage. The car would be returned after the dues along with the strong-arm recovery charges were cleared. The system worked well. If the taxi driver were diligent, the loan could be paid off and the taxi would be his. The interest rates were a little high. At 20%, it was well above the government stipulated rate of 12%. For a man with limited assets, wanting to start a tourist taxi service, there were few options.

A tourist taxi got custom if the driver developed a reputation for honest reliability. This reputation would spread by word of mouth. Biju had cultivated a group of regular customers who trusted him. Whenever Alicekutty's husband came in from the Middle East, Biju would be given a call. He would pick up the man from the airport and take him home. There would be further visits to friends and family. There would be no haggling about the fare. Occasionally, if his taxi were not free, he would make arrangements with another hired car. This was the extent of his responsibility. Biju's tag of dependability ensured that his cab never lay idle.

Contrary to public perception, tourist taxi drivers are responsible drivers and good citizens. They constantly came to each other's aid. It was common for Bijumon to stop by the wayside, diverting traffic from a road block ahead. Sometimes he would stop by the wayside to warn other cabs about a surprise check of documents by some extortive motor vehicle authority. Biju had a tough life. He slept late and would get up early. The money however was good and his loan repayments never lapsed.

Chapter 2   Biju Immigrates.

Biju's taxi was almost two years old when Biju was offered a job abroad. There was a regular customer of his, a construction engineer who had migrated to Dubai. He offered to get Biju a job in his firm as a fire safety officer. Would Biju be interested? Biju was in two minds.

Jobs in the Middle East were opportunities to raise some capital. Most aspirants proceeded through an agent. The agents charged a heavy fee and also kept part of the remuneration. They duped their clients in every way they could. The men worked as bonded labour. There were no laws in the Middle East to prevent the exploitation of immigrant workers. They were exploited and looted by their agents and poorly treated by the local populace.

Biju remembered the story of an engineer from near his village who had gone with his young wife to one of the oil sheikdoms. They had taken a cab from the airport to a hotel. On the way, the driver had asked the man to get down and to buy some refreshments. When the man returned from the store, the car with his wife had disappeared. She must have ended up in some sheik's harem.

The horror stories were innumerable. Besides, Biju had married recently. His wife Shija was expecting their first child. Biju's friends also dissuaded him. Life in these countries was expensive. Besides, one had to have discipline. One could not take a day off or not shave. Shoes and a belt were compulsory and punctuality was insisted upon.

What finally convinced Biju was the advice given by his wife. Their taxi was getting old. By the time the loan payments were completed, it would not be reliable anymore. They would then need to take a new loan to buy another vehicle. The cycle of penury would never end. Shija was sure that Biju would do well in the Middle East. He was diligent and had no vices.

When Biju reached Dubai, he reported to his agent at the airport. The agent instructed him to wait. About fifteen immigrant workers for the agency would be coming in that day. Once all of them reached, a vehicle would take them to their barracks where they would be housed. A flight from Bangladesh had come in with ten workers. Another four were expected from Pakistan in an hour's time.

The van left with its load of immigrants. The city of Dubai was grander than any he had ever seen. The van was air conditioned. The dormitory accommodation allotted to the migrant workers was air conditioned. In the earlier days they used to keep immigrant workers in tin sheds. Dubai however was aiming at being not only an economic, but also a tourist hub. Image was important. Apparent squalor would spoil the image.

For a hundred Dirhams a month, workers could also get two nutritious meals a day from the hostel. Most immigrant unskilled workers were paid around six to seven hundred Dirhams a month. It would leave them with monthly savings of about four hundred Dirhams which they would transfer to their families back home.

The minimum wages in the sheikdom was fixed by law to be fifteen hundred Dirhams a month. Immigrant workers however were beneath the law. No one bothered about these foreigners from poor countries. It was traditional and acceptable to exploit third world workers. Empires through the ages have been built by slave labour.

Chapter 3   Biju starts Work

Biju's sponsor had ensured that he did not get fleeced by any agent. Now it was up to him to prove his enterprise. There could be no cronyism at the workplace. After all, his sponsor too was an immigrant, albeit in a supervisory grade.

Biju was up at four in the morning. At five in the morning, the company bus would pick him up with the others. On reaching the construction site, Biju was asked to report to the security officer. The security officer was a burly Pathan, Suleiman Sheikh. He asked Biju about his previous experience in fire and safety duties. Biju had obtained his certificate from an agency by paying Rupees Five Thousand. He had no clue about what his duties entailed. He told Suleiman the truth. The security man was pleased. Many of the others had tried to bluff their way. Biju was honest at the very least.

Bijumon was given the job of distributing helmets and harnesses to the labour force when they checked in, in the morning. He would collect the safety gear back after each shift. During the day, he would drive Suleiman around the construction site. Suleiman taught him what hazards to look for and how to pull up people who flouted safety norms.

The construction company was building a hypermarket complex outside the city. It was rumoured that the financer and owner of the complex was Sheik Iqbal, kingpin of the gangs that terrorized wealthy industrialists and filmmakers in the city of Mumbai. At Dubai however Iqbal was above the law. He was a man of great respect and prestige. His business interests in the Sheikdom and in the rest of the world were crackling clean and above board.

Sheik Iqbal did not visit the construction site often. That was the advantage of being a man of respect. Nobody would cut corners in Iqbal's projects.

A year went by. Suleiman was giving Biju more and more responsibilities. Biju was on security duties at the construction site when a large black limousine flanked by two security jeeps with armed men inside drew up at the barricade. He had received no instructions from Suleiman to let anyone in. Biju refused to raise the barricade.

Two burly armed men got out of the first jeep, obviously furious. One of them stepped forward to swipe Biju with the butt of his rifle, when a call from the Limousine stopped him.

Sheikh Iqbal stepped out. The man was around Biju's height, but stockily built. His cold gimlet eyes exuded power. Looking at him one would hardly suspect that the millionaires of Mumbai would break out in a cold sweat at the mere mention of his name.

Suleiman' jeep had drawn up inside the gate. He rushed forward profusely apologizing to Iqbal on the indignity of having been stopped outside his own property. He turned to Biju. "I will teach you a lesson. From tomorrow I will have you sweeping the floor at the construction site" he said. Biju was petrified. If he was sent back to India, he would be ruined. His taxi had been sold and he did not have the resources to buy another.

Iqbal beckoned Biju to step up. Biju stepped forward and saluted like how Suleiman had taught him. Iqbal looked him up and down. Biju half expected him to whip out a pistol and shoot him in the head. It would be better than the disgrace of going back empty handed, he thought. He braced himself for the worst. Iqbal's next words surprised him. "Good man. You do your duty well. I will take you in my security detail" he said. "Don't worry", he added, seeing a look of consternation appear on Biju's face. "I am not making you join my gang. My boys in Bombay do all that. Your job will be whistle clean". Suleiman was vigorously nodding his head. Biju accepted. "Good" said Iqbal. "Get into the jeep".

Biju was sent to United Kingdom for an advanced security and anti-terrorist course. This would involve a year's training on the state-of-the-art security systems and counter terrorist measures. During his course, he would receive a stipend of seven thousand Dirhams. After he finished his course, the remuneration would be much higher.

The training capsule was conducted by M18 operatives and attended by police and antiterrorist operatives from all over the world. Biju had been chosen by Iqbal for the course, as his name had not been associated with any organization with terror connections.

Officially, Biju had been detailed by the government of Dubai. He learned everything about weaponry and communications. He also learned how to operate a speed boat and to fly a helicopter. The course was intensive and time whizzed past. He would be returning to Dubai soon. Officially he would be part of the Dubai police force. In actuality he would be looking after Iqbal's security.

It had been two years since Biju left home. He had son in Kerala who was eighteen months old whom he had never seen. He wanted to visit his family before taking up his appointment at Dubai. Iqbal agreed. There was one condition however. Biju would bring his wife and son back with him to Dubai when he returned in a month. A suitable house with all the facilities would be waiting for them. Iqbal's generosity was genuine. With his family there, Biju's loyalty would be ironclad.

Chapter 5   Biju visits Home

Bijumon was a wealthy man now. Without his knowledge Iqbal's organization had been remitting money into his account every month. His son Shibu, was an exact replica of the father. Biju told Shija that they could move with him with him to Dubai. She was a little surprised. Only the very affluent of immigrants could afford to take their families with them. Shija had never been out of Kerala before and she had never travelled by air. She looked forward to the adventure.

Biju was soon busy tying up loose ends at home. He made arrangements with a local bank for transferring money into his parent's account every month. He also bought them a car and arranged a driver for them. There were repairs on the house to be done. The boundary wall had to be fenced. The month of leave went by fast. It was time for him to go back.

A large contingent of their family and relatives had come to the airport to see him off. He remembered his first trip to Dubai. He had landed up at the international airport alone, lugging his suitcase.

Now that he was prosperous, his popularity rating had shot up.

The air tickets had been bought by Iqbal's organization and he was traveling first class. Biju was happy that his family could experience this opulence, which was beyond the reach of most immigrants. It was a far cry from the crammed economy class.

The hostess was courteous and the passengers could choose their cuisine. An air hostess gifted Shibu with a small replica of the plane they were flying on. The boy was thrilled.

When they reached Dubai, they exited by a separate ramp. This ramp was exclusively for the first-class passengers.

A Mercedes sedan with its uniformed chauffer was waiting for them. Their baggage had already been collected. There was a two storied bungalow that had been readied for him near Iqbal's palace. The bungalow had its own thermal controlled swimming pool. High walls surrounded the courtyard. It was unbecoming to allow your neighbours glimpses into your private property.

The city of Dubai was like any other city in the west. The cars were posh and the roads swank. There were men in traditional Arab robes and women in

Burkah. There were also an equal number of men and women in western attire. They were given two days to see the sights around Dubai before Biju joined work. Shija insisted on wearing a sari. She would have to get used to western or Arabic attire later.

There was a time when wearing a sari was almost a prestige symbol in the Middle East. Those days only the royalty and the affluent in India could afford to travel abroad. With the influx of a large number of Indian health care workers into the Middle East, sari clad women started to be looked down upon. The era of rich Indian Princes and Princesses coming for tourism was over.

Chapter 6   Biju learns his new Job.

It took Biju almost a month to learn the working of the Iqbal business empire. Iqbal had a chain of multiplex complexes and shopping malls in Dubai. He hired these out to local and multinational agencies. Iqbal was directly involved in the jewellery business and had a string of outlets in the Middle East and Europe.

Biju visited their jewellery fabrication centre. There were Egyptian craftsmen working with high end technology to create some of the most magnificent masterpieces he had ever seen. Biju was given the overall task of supervising the security apparatus. He had a small army of security men working for him. They established a control centre which monitored the security of all Iqbal's establishments centrally.

The crime rate in Dubai was low. Draconian Islamic laws were a powerful deterrent to shoplifters and thieves. In Europe, jewellery outlets depended on close circuit TV's and alarm systems. The high tech security apparatus was wired into the local police control room. Police in western Europe were efficient and effective. They could depend on them for security.

It was a different story in India. All the basic gadgetry was installed, but considered redundant. The name of Iqbal Sheikh invoked such terror that elaborate and expensive security tie ups were dispensed with. Only a fool would attempt to steal from Sheik Iqbal.

Biju's most delicate task was to provide security cover to the great Sheikh Iqbal himself. There were rival gangs and even a few national security agencies that would love to eliminate this visionary. As a friend of the crown prince, Iqbal enjoyed diplomatic immunity in and around the Middle East. Hired guns and lone operatives could be used without a tell-tale trail. Biju was always on guard against suicidal field agents.

Biju's team had the best of armoured limousines. Theirs was an elite squad of security agents drawn from the commando units of various countries. The most crucial element however was the security of information. When Iqbal travelled abroad, Biju was one of the few men who knew his itinerary. Iqbal usually travelled under an alias. There would be decoys attending various functions elsewhere. Disguised and plains clothes security men forged impenetrable cordons.

Iqbal's greatest security asset was his men's devotion to him. He had the rare gift of earning the loyalty of his men. Many of his men would willingly die to protect him. Biju was however, always a little wary of the Indian gang leaders who came to call on Iqbal. They were carefully but unobtrusively screened before being admitted into Iqbal's presence. Iqbal himself was blasé about his security. He had lived by the gun in his Bombay days. He always maintained that he would rather die by a bullet than be smothered by a crowd of doctors on a hospital bed.

Chapter 7   Iqbal's Vision

When Shibu was five years old, he started attending the international school. Shija had adjusted well to her life in Dubai. She was the women's secretary of the Indian association. There were cultural activities. Social evenings had to be arranged for visiting dignitaries and priests.

Dubai was also a hot destination for the Bollywood stars. If they came to Dubai and did a couple of performances, they could earn quite a packet. This money was not taxed and could be stashed away in a Swiss bank account of their choice.

Iqbal Sheikh was now going old. There was a lot of pressure on him and the stress was taking its toll. There had been an extradition attempt by the Indian government after a politically sensitive hit by the Bombay gang. Iqbal did not control the activities of the Bombay gang directly.

The errors of judgment by his lieutenants at Bombay saddened him. He travelled less and less. In Dubai, he was safe. But if he travelled abroad there could be trouble. He spent more time with his family now. His wife was a devout Muslim. His sons were involved in the running of the family empire, but he did not trust their judgment.

The regional heads of Iqbal's organization met every month at Dubai. The meeting would be on the terrace of Dubai's famous Bejois de Arab. Delegates from all parts of the world would be picked up by helicopters from the airport and ferried to the hotel's rooftop helipad. There were presentations, discussions and personal interactions. This was where Iqbal assessed the performance of his teams and the calibre and character of his associates.

There would be detailed descriptions and analyses. Figures would be presented, but more importantly, Iqbal got an opportunity to look into the eyes of his men. He could identify treachery and failure at a glance.

The Indian operation was facing rough weather. For decades there had been pressure on the Bombay police to crack down on Iqbal's gangs in Bombay. Iqbal himself had been urging his boys to move out of strong arm and extortion into legitimate business. The Indian economy was booming and fortunes could be made without recourse to violence. Unfortunately, his men were short sighted. There was an endless stream of hit men from the neighboring states. It was easier to skim the cream off a business man's earnings. Besides they had no patience or experience in business management.

After one of these monthly meets, Iqbal invited Biju and Shija home. Shibu had gone for his riding lessons and would be picked up later by their housekeeper. While the ladies sat in the perfumed garden Iqbal discussed the future with Biju. Iqbal wanted Biju to set up a business house in India. The funding would be organized through the Dubai international bank. They would recruit talented youngsters to run the venture. The financial men they hired would work out the details. Iqbal looked at Biju. Was Biju willing and ready for this new initiative?

Biju was a little wary. The new enterprise could become a target for rival gangs. He would prefer to keep his family in the safety of Dubai. Iqbal smiled. He had anticipated this response from Biju. There was a palm shaped group of Island villas being constructed off the Dubai coast. Iqbal had an interest in some of them. The security there was foolproof. He would earmark one villa for Biju's family.

Shija had no intention of staying on at Dubai with Biju at Bombay. If Biju was shifting base, she would like to be in India too. If Biju felt that Bombay was not safe for his family, she could stay at Kerala with his parents. Shibu's education however would be better in Europe. They decided to send Shibu to a residential public school at Switzerland. Over the next six months Shibu finalized the plans.

The mobile phone revolution was taking India by storm. The new company would choose this sector as an opening for investment. They planned to diversify later into other areas. Electronic goods, cosmetics, designer garments and other lifestyle products were on the agenda.

Iqbal's group bought the controlling interest in a mobile phone company based in Singapore. Then they set up a branch at Bombay and started their operations. Biju hired a group of bright business school graduates in his team. They bought the rights to an emerging technology for phones. This innovation prevented hand held phones from heating up even after prolonged use. A series of 'Cool' phones was launched. 'Cool Phones' soon became a rage in the metros. Biju's first business venture was soon a grand success.

A week after the launch of 'Cool Phones', a young man walked into Biju's office and demanded twenty lakh rupees. He claimed to represent Iqbal Bhai. Biju was amused. He told the man to return the next day. Biju made a phone call to Iqbal's secretary.

The next morning the young man landed up with two accomplices to collect the money. Iqbal's men were waiting. They caught the men and took them away. These crooks provided information on other gangs which were operating in Iqbal's name. A minor cleansing of the crime world was set in motion by Iqbal's men. The smaller gangs were decimated. Biju regretted not having acquiesced to the young man's demand. He could have avoided a blood bath.

Shija had settled comfortably in Kerala. They had constructed a new house at the outskirts of Kottayam. It had been done tastefully without being ostentatious. Biju's parents had moved in with Shija into the new house. Shija started a house for orphan children after acquiring a broken-down hospital premises. They picked up destitute children from all over the state. With its staff of caretakers and teachers in place, the orphanage soon exceeded its projected capacity of thirty children.

At Christmas, when Shibu's school closed for two months, Biju and Shija went to pick him up. They had a holiday in Europe before coming to Kerala where they spend a month. The youth was shaping up well. He excelled in his studies. His stated ambition was to become a doctor. They had a great time at Kerala too. The boy was proud of his roots and mopped up all the information like a greedy sponge. Then it was time for Shibu to return to his studies.

Chapter 9   Another Meeting.

Cool phones had diversified. There were now popular ranges of 'Cool TVs', 'Air Conditioners' and Cool Refrigerators. A range of summer wear called 'Summer Cool' was launched with much fanfare and soon became a rage. Iqbal had got a full return on his investment.

Money poured in. Biju continued to divert half the profits into Iqbal's Dubai account. The other half was kept for R&D and for launching new products. Ten years went by. The 'Cool' range now included computers, two wheelers and holiday resorts. Shibu was doing his premedical education at London. Shija now had more than a hundred children in her 'Centre for the underprivileged'. She had also started an old age home for those who had no families to stay with after retirement. These were the folks who had been orphaned by age. There was a strong sense of community amongst the inmates. The members themselves would take care of others who were sick and cheer up those who were going through a bad patch. The concept and it's implementation were uniquely successful. Shija had shifted to Mumbai to be with Biju. She still controlled and continued to pay monthly visits to the establishments she had set up.

Biju had attended one of the monthly meets of the organization at Dubai. As he was leaving, Iqbal asked him to stay back. Biju knew that the boss had some other task for him. He phoned up Shija to tell her that he had to stay back in Dubai for a day. That evening Biju went to Iqbal's house. Iqbal put his arm around Biju and walked with him in the garden. Biju immediately sensed that something was wrong. The arm around him was not any more out of camaraderie. It was out of a physical need for support. Biju now noted that Iqbal was pale and a little breathless. Iqbal's once powerful arm which was resting around his shoulders was frail now.

Biju's fears were soon confirmed. Iqbal had bad news for him. The Sheik was suffering from a cancer of the prostate gland. The disease had spread to his bones. The doctors had told him that he had only a few months to live. He was worried about his sons. They had no vision. Without Iqbal, the organization would soon deteriorate into an extortion gang once again.

Iqbal was looking at Biju for suggestions. Biju had none to offer. If Iqbal's sons wanted to take over the 'Cool' assets, he would willingly accede. Iqbal nodded. He had expected Biju to say that. He only wished that Biju had been his son.

Chapter 10   Shija moves to London

Biju returned to Mumbai. Shibu had been unwell for the past few months. Shija worried that he was studying too hard and not eating enough. They had acquired a small apartment outside London. She wished to stay there for a while. Shibu could then stay at home and have hot meals when he returned from his classes.

Biju agreed. They flew down to London. Shihu had lost weight. Biju settled Shija and Shibu in their apartment and returned to Bombay.

Iqbal's health deteriorated faster than expected. He was soon on his deathbed. Biju was called to Dubai again. Iqbal's house had been converted into a mini hospital. There was a specialist doctor and a few nurses in attendance. Iqbal was on heavy doses of pain killers and the medication made him drowsy. When the medication wore off, his body would be wracked by painful spasms.

Biju was seated by his side, when he breathed his last. He had held Biju's hand with an unexpectedly strong grip. They looked into each others eye. The grip on Biju's hand slackened and Iqbal seemed to sigh. He breathed his last. The era of Iqbal was over.

The next day, there was a state funeral for him. That same evening the sons called for Biju. Iqbal's prediction was right. The sons wanted control of 'Cool Industries'. They advised Biju to retire.

Biju had been prepared for this. He had brought with him, a copy of the company's asset and balance sheets. In three days, he handed over the reins of the company he created. He flew to London to join Shija. Shibu would now have both parents to return to, in the evenings.

Shibu had been having a hacking cough now for over six months. An X-ray of his chest done earlier had shown a small lesion in one of the lungs. They put him through a whole battery of tests including a bronchoscopy. When the results came, the doctors were happy. They had suspected a cancer. But the results of the investigations were all negative.

It was decided that the boy had possibly contacted a tubercular infection during one of his visits to India. They started him on anti-tubercular treatment. Shibu was advised to take it easy for a semester. After six months, when the course of treatment was complete, he could return to mainstream academics.

With Shija's home cooking and the medication, Shibu showed good improvement. He put on some weight and the color came back to his cheeks. Shija had got some Ayurvedic medicines from a doctor in

Kerala, which she gave Shibu along with his tuberculosis treatment.

The six months of treatment were complete. Biju and Shija took their son to hospital for a check up before stopping the TB drugs. A fresh CT scan of the chest was ordered. When the results came, they were in for a shock. The disease had spread. The boy needed admission in hospital.

With further tests there was even worse news. There was evidence of disease now all over the body. There were shadows in the MR scans of his brain. There were nodules in his liver. The doctors held a conference. This was not Tuberculosis. There must be a cancer which was producing this dramatic radiological deterioration.

Shibu's liver lesion was biopsied. When the results came in it the worst fears were confirmed. The tissue showed features of a malignancy. They still could not ascertain where the tumour had originated. That was however only of academic interest. The disease was beyond any hope of cure.

The downhill course of the disease was rapid. Shibu never came out of hospital again. He died within a month. They buried him after a farewell prayer at the university chapel.

Shija was inconsolable. She had hardly eaten anything since her son got admitted. Her life had revolved round her son's achievements. And she slid now into a deep depression. Bijumon was constantly with her.

Shija refused to go back to Kerala without her son. Biju tried to console her. He consulted the best doctors. There was a resort at Goa, run by a psychiatrist where many patients in depression had been helped. Biju went with her to the resort.

The resort was run by the church. There would be prayers in the morning. The psychiatrist would then visit all the patients and decide on any changes in medication. There were group exercises and activities. The afternoons were free. Family members were encouraged to be with their wards at this time. They could go for walks in the garden or visit the library. Biju did everything he could.

 Every ten odd days Shija would show some improvement. Then she would settle into her closed world of sorrow again. The psychiatrist who was treating her was optimistic. It was a grief reaction. Given time and love she would come out of it. He was horribly wrong.

One evening Biju got worried. Shija had been in the bathroom too long. He knocked at the door. There was no response. He kicked the door open and went in. She was lying in the bath tub. She was dead. She had slashed both wrists with a razor blade.

Biju got her buried at the Goa cathedral. He needed a week to tie up his affairs. He made an endowment. Most of his assets were donated to an organization which helped children with cancer.

A few days later, the old age home that Shija had set up had a visitor. No one recognized the new inmate as he signed in at the register. He signed in as Bijumon, previous occupation- immigrant worker. He had reached the end of his journey.

Chapter 12   The Affair

She had rushed into the train as it was pulling out of the platform. She was well built and tall, not pretty but with strong features that suggested character. This was the Venad express, a train that commuters used daily, to return home from work. Most of the passengers were regulars. They saw each other in the morning and evening in the train, jostled each other for seats yet never spoke to one another. It is the ethos of today's world. There is no time for introductions.

The lady, let us call her Rekha for the lack of a better tag was obviously not a regular on this route. She had picked up her mobile and was speaking to someone. There was some rescheduling of plans. She would be a little late as she had missed the Alleppy train. Her house, I could gather, was somewhere between the two routes. The Venad would suffice. The telephone messages had been passed. There was something else that troubled her. She looked at me, an obvious stranger to these parts and looked away again. There was a youth sitting near the window. She tapped him on the shoulder. "Can you buy a ticket for me to Kayamkulam at the next station"? The next station was the 'Ernakulam

Junction' and the train would halt there for about fifteen minutes.

The ticket counter however was a distance away. There would be Queues at the counter. It was not an easy proposition. If she had asked me for the favor I would have had to decline. If the train left before I could get back, I would have no option but to take a bus. The roads were winding and bumpy and the bus would be packed.

The youth looked at the lady. I was certain that he would refuse. Malayalee boys are not particularly known for their chivalry. I was also taken aback by the lady's confidence in herself. A lady in a similar predicament in north India would never have the courage to ask a stranger for help. She would be putting herself in real danger.

The youth hesitated, then nodded his head and left his seat. I was not sure if he would come back. He could have easily shifted to another compartment, away from irritating females who asked for undue favours. It was also possible that his journey destination was the terminus itself. I could see that the lady was sharing the same concerns. The train was filling up. She kept her bag next to her to keep a seat for him. Furtively, she kept glancing out of the window.

He came back, just as the train was leaving. His sweaty shirt clung to a well-proportioned physique. He obviously had had to run to make it back on time. Rekha was grateful. She paid him and took the ticket. She made room next to herself. He sat down, careful not to touch her. The train was moving now. Rekha fidgeted restlessly. She wanted to thank him, but did not want to appear brash. Rekha, like many of the women of Kerala was confident. Kerala is a good place for women. Female infanticide is almost unheard of. There was no danger of molestation in public places or in public transport. Women could work with dignity.

She turned to the youth and asked him his name. His name was Raj. She asked him where he was going and what he did for a living. He responded initially in monosyllables and later with more enthusiasm. He was responding to her warmth, but appeared rather uncomfortable. Raj did not want to seem the type who struck up conversations with the fairer sex in trains.

The train stopped at another station. Another youth of Raj's acquaintance got in. He raised his eyebrows on seeing Raj conversing with a lady. Raj got up and moved with his friend to near the train door, a popular place for young commuters. Another lady who had got in occupied the youth's place. A middle-aged man sitting across smirked, expressing resentment at Raj's youth and at the attention Rekha was paying him. The train reached Kottayam.

This was one of the larger stations in this route. Many passengers would be detraining. There were two window seats vacant now. The youths came back and sat opposite each other. Rekha got up from her seat and moved next to Raj. She was peeved and intrigued by his apparent disinterest. She started the conversation again. They talked about each other and about regional politics. After a while the other youth moved off. He could sense that he was intruding on a private affair. Their body language belied the obvious chemistry they had evolved.

Chengannurs station was drawing near. Rekha would have to get off. The youth escorted her to the compartment door. They waited at the platform together, communicating in eloquent silence. The train whistle blew. Raj would have to get on again. They held hands for a moment. Their shoulders brushed as he turned back into the coach and then the train moved on. Rekha walked off the platform and to the parking lot. Her husband was waiting for her outside with his motorbike. She hopped on behind him and then they were off.

Shakuni the Boatwoman

Chapter 1   *Shakuni*

Shakuni was the boat woman at the ferry point next to the rubber factory. It was a rather unusual profession for a woman. Circumstances had demanded it. Her father Chandran had been appointed the ferry man by an earlier politician. Chandran had the necessary credentials. His house was next to the river and he had a boat. The government would pay him two thousand rupees every month for managing the ferry.

The money was not much. The nature of him job fitted in with his life. It was very convenient. Commuters would come to the ferry point which was next to his hut. He would ferry them across to the other side from where they could cut across to town through the Kottayam market. There would be a continuous stream of people in the morning and evening hours. The rest of the time he was free.

He could use that time to do odd jobs around his house or to tend to his cows and ducks. Milking the cows had been his job till his daughter turned ten years of age. She then took over the milking. She would deliver this milk to the four or five affluent houses in the locality. They made more money selling milk and the duck's eggs than what the government paid them for manning the ferry.

When Shakuni was small, she still needed her father's help for bathing the cows and pushing them out to the pasture. The ducks were easier to manage. It was easier to herd them quacking into the paddy fields, where they would swim around catching insects. Shakuni had a brother who had fallen on his head when he was a baby. At least that was what everyone said. He was more difficult to manage than the cows and the ducks and definitely less capable of looking after himself.

Shakuni's brothers name was Ramu and he was mentally subnormal. He could not speak and he walked with a peculiar stiff gait. He communicated his needs by grunts and elaborate gestures. Ramu shuffled around aimlessly most of the day. Chandran and Shakuni worried that he would one day fall into the river and drown.

Shakuni's brother was five years younger than her. Her mother had died soon after her brother was born. Chandran considered himself blessed to have a daughter like Shakuni. For the first few years after her mother's death, Shakuni's grandmother had stayed with them. By the time Shakuni was eight however, her grandma shifted back to her own house. Shakuni had learned the ropes fast. By the time she was ten years old, her father had handed over the responsibility of looking after her retarded brother to Shakuni. With the cows and ducks and a challenged brother, Shakuni had her hands full. The question of attending school never arose.

Chapter 2   Shakuni grows up

Chandran had one vice. He had a weakness for toddy. It had started as a nightly tot. By the time Shakuni was fifteen, Chandran was almost always drunk. He never misbehaved or fought with anyone. He would start the day with a bottle and keep at it till sundown. Soon, Chandran could no longer be relied upon to get the boat across the river safely. Shakuni took over that job also.

In the first few days there were a few stares. Soon everyone got used a boat woman ferrying them across the river. It required strength to pull the boat across through the tangled mesh of weeds that clogged the river. When the rains came, the weeds were purged into the great lake. Now the overflowing river had treacherous currents. It was a man's job, but Shakuni was man enough. She had been born by the river and could swim like a fish. Shakuni handled the boat as well as any man.

Chandran's liver gave in when Shakuni was eighteen. He had vomited blood and had been rushed to hospital. His face was as pale as a sack of cement. His tummy was bloated like a drowned cow's carcass. For a week he had hovered between life and death. Occasionally he would wake up and ask for a bottle of toddy. One morning his breathing became heavy and his eyes turned a pale yellow. The next morning, he was dead. After his death, Shakuni applied for the job of ferrywoman. She got it as there were no other applicants.

Her brother was an asset now. His presence at home added a semblance of security for Shakuni. It would have been improper for her to stay alone in the hut otherwise. He was easier to manage now and would not venture near the river's edge. He would even help with a few jobs like the feeding of the ducks.

The day began early for Shakuni. She had to milk and feed the cows. Then she would deliver the milk and shepherd the ducks to the pond before the first commuters arrived at the ferry point. She would make Ramu sit by the paddy field's edge to scare away any stray dogs that might get after the ducks. The next two hours would be hard work. There was a rope stretched from edge to edge, to help pull the boat across the river. When her arms were sore, she would use the boatman's pole, a long bamboo stalk to push her ferry boat.

After the passengers were all ferried, she would get the ducks back to their enclosure and then set about cooking for the day. In the evening as people returned from town, the ferry would start again. There was a lamppost outside their house. That and a kerosene lamp would provide enough light for the house as dusk rolled in.

Another couple of years went by. The crowds for the ferry were thinner now. A new bridge had been made a couple of kilometres downriver and a government owned bus now plied the route. Then one day she received a note from the municipality. The government would not finance the ferry anymore.

Milk was now available in tetra packs from an outlet nearby. Fortunately, a hotel in the locality agreed to let her supply milk and eggs daily. They paid well below the market price, but the money was regular.

Chapter 3   Ramu's Accident

One day, she was coming after delivering the day's batch of eggs to the hotel when she heard a commotion by the duck pond. She ran to the field's edge. Ramu was not to be seen. A small crowd of people had collected on the adjacent road and were pointing towards the pond and shouting. No one ventured into the pond. Fully clothed, she jumped in to look for her brother. The duck pond was an abandoned paddy field. The pond itself was not deep. In a corner of the submerged field there was a treacherous well.

Ramu's stick, which he used to scare away stray dogs, was floating on the surface of the pond. Shakuni tried to dive into the well. It was too deep for her. The water was too murky to see anything. Exhausted and crying she gave up.

A day later Ramu's body floated up. Shakuni spent the little money that she had for her brothers final rites. She sold off her ducks and the two calves to the hotel owner for a throw away price. Shakuni then took a bus to her grandparent's house.

Her grandmother was the only person in the house who seemed happy to see her. Her maternal uncle who was staying there with his family looked worried. His aunt and her two daughters were downright hostile.

Shakuni had received two thousand rupees she had received on selling her livestock. She handed over the money to her uncle. She wanted to stay with them for a month. She would sleep on the floor next to grandmother's bed. She would also help with the cooking and cleaning. In a month's time she would have secured some job for herself in the town and would move out. It seemed a fair deal. Her uncle agreed.

In the morning after the cooking and dish washing were complete, she set out job hunting. Every evening, she came back home disappointed. The only jobs she was offered was as a housemaid. That would be a dead end. The money would not be enough and the work would be too binding for her to later try for another job.

Twenty days were over. There were rumblings from her aunt that she was not trying hard enough. She even suggested that Shakuni go back and stay by the river alone.

Her grandmother was glad to have Shakuni around. She was old now and could do with a little help. Her daughter in law and grand daughters were not too keen to do any errands for her.

On the twenty first day, Shakuni was getting ready to leave on her job hunt when her grandmother called her. Could she warm some water for her bath? Shakuni was in a fix. The bus to town would be leaving soon. Quickly, she got the water ready for her.

Shakuni ran to the bus stop. Her bus had left. Fortunately, another bus was drawing up. Shakuni ran forward waving her hands. The bus stopped for her and she hopped in. This bus was less crowded than the one she normally took. There was an empty seat and she gratefully sat on it. It would take an hour for the bus to reach town.

She closed her eyes and prayed fervently that she would get a job today. She dozed off. The bus conductor was sitting and tabulating yesterday's fares. The bus was not crowded and he would have to give the accounts when he reached the terminus. The tabulations were complete. There were a couple more tickets to be issued. He took his time before he finally ambled up to her.

Shakuni opened her eyes when the conductor tapped her shoulder. "Town stop", she told him, handing him the fare of five rupees. She opened her eyes. The conductor was not taking her money. He was looking at her in a funny way. She looked outside. The scenery was unfamiliar. "Do you know which bus you are on?" the conductor was asking her. Shakuni told him the truth that she could not read.

The conductor rang the bell for the bus to stop. "Get off here. If you wait by that gate on the other side you will get a bus to take you back". The conductor looked at his watch. "The next bus will come in about an hour", he told her firmly. A dejected Shakuni got off the bus. She crossed the road. Another day had been wasted. It was a hopeless situation. She sat down near the gate and cried.

About fifteen minutes passed. A car drew up outside the gate. The chauffer wore a white shirt and cap. A middle-aged lady with an authoritative air and her daughter sat in the back seat. The girl was coming home after completing her first semester of engineering. Her mother, Mrs Varma, headmistress of the Seagull residential school for girls, had gone to the airport to pick her up.

The driver stopped the car and got out to open the gate. He yelled at Shakuni who was sitting there. "Get up. Can't you see that you are blocking the gate"? Shakuni scurried away to one side. Mrs Varma looked at Shakuni and then looked away. The driver was back in the car now. The young girl Shikha, tugged at her mother's sleeve. "She is crying mama. Please ask her what happened".

Mrs Varma looked around. There was no one in sight. She asked the driver to call Shakuni over and asked her who she was and what she was doing at the Seagull school gate. Shakuni told her about the wrong bus that she had taken. "Get into the car", Mrs. Verma told her. "The school van will be going to town to buy provisions for the week in about one hour. I will send you to town in that".

Chapter 4   Providence

They drove into the sprawling campus of the Seagull school. Mrs Verma asked Shakuni about herself. Shakuni told her the whole story. She told her about her brother's death and how she had landed up at her Grand-mother's place. When they reached the principal's bungalow, the driver stopped the car. Mrs Verma called the driver aside.

"The girl's story is too melodramatic. She must be up to some mischief. Send her off to town in the van quickly before she steals something". Mrs Verma, like most school principals was suspicious by design.. The driver came up in Shakuni's defence. He was not one to contradict his mistress very often. His conscience was pricking him today.

"Madam" he pleaded, "I did not recognize the girl earlier. As she spoke, I recognized her. All that she said is true. I have crossed the river in her ferry and have seen her brother". Shikha had been listening to everything. There were tears in her eyes. She pleaded with her mother to give Shakuni a peon's job.

Mrs Verma hesitated. She hated impulsive decision making. Yet, her daughter's compassion pleased her. "All right", she told the driver. "Ask her to wait in the porch. I will interview her after breakfast". She called out to the kitchen maid and gave her instructions. "Shikha has come from the IIT. Lay out the breakfast. There is a young lady sitting in the porch. Give her some tea and biscuits".

Shakuni thus got appointed as the chief janitor of the Seagull Girls Residential School. It was her job to keep the school and residential premises clean. The school had been closed for summer vacations. It would reopen again in another week. There was a small house next to the principal's bungalow which was given to Shakuni. Mrs. Varma also loaned her some money to buy provisions and bed sheets. She would have to settle down in a couple of days. Then the school girls would be coming in after their holidays.

Shakuni was an eager and able worker. She was always early to the school. Every day when the girls trooped out of their dormitories and into class, the rooms would be spick and span. Boards would be wiped clean and a fresh stock of chalks ready. Then Shakuni would set about sorting out the mess in the dorms. She showed so much enthusiasm that she was soon very popular with the students and all the staff.

Miss Elliot, the English teacher offered to take special evening classes for her. Shakuni jumped for joy. Her education had started. The girls in school also got into the spirit of things. They were thrilled to have a student. After dinner, when they had free time, they would tutor Shakuni, plying her with information on everything from alphabets to atoms and algebra to advanced economics. Six months after she had been appointed Shikha got a letter from Shakuni, in English, thanking her for her love and compassion. A new life was starting for her with the opportunities Shikha had given her. Shikha was so moved by the letter that she cried over it for a good while. She started corresponding regularly with Shakuni. She had always wanted a sister and now she had one.

When Shikha came home for vacations, Shakuni was there at the airport with Mrs. Verma. Dressed in a smart 'Salwar Kameez', she looked more like a college student than a Janitor.

Chapter 5   Graduation Time

Shakuni's education progressed. The Kerala government had launched a new scheme to encourage education amongst women. Women were permitted to sit for their tenth examinations without attending formal school. They had to however clear a preliminary examination held by the board. Shakuni was a fast learner. Within a year of starting her education, Shakuni had cleared her tenth and was soon preparing for her twelfth examination.

Shikha was specializing in computer science. She encouraged Shakuni to learn computers. She would send Sakuni e-mails on the school computer, to which Shakuni would reply. After some time, she started sending her some assignments too, which Shakuni would struggle to complete. By the time Shakuni passed her twelfth examinations, she was also well versed in computer applications. Mrs. Verma appointed her as the principal's secretary.

Shikha was finishing her engineering course. She qualified and then opted to enter the Indian Administrative service. Her mother had tried to dissuade her. The civil services looked powerful and glamorous from the outside. But she had heard of the internal machinations. She had her ex-students within the organization. They told her of the tribulations and frustrations that a dedicated officer had to face. Mrs. Verma had not been favourably impressed.

Promotions and appointments within the organization depended on the confidential reports or CR's you received from your seniors. These CR's were based on selfish perceptions and rankled with favouritism. As the officers grew more senior the politicians called the shots. Few administrative service officers could work for their conscience.

Shika had however made up her mind. A boy she liked, who had been her senior at the institute had joined the Indian Police Service. He spoke in glowing terms of the quality of life. The civil service was a legacy of the British Raj. A Raj that had lost its public-school sheen and flavour, Mrs. Verma would affirm.

The young rarely listen to their parent's advice. Shikha listened to her mother. She had made up her mind. With her sharp mind and astute preparation, she did well in the civil services selection examination. The training period was all idealism and values. Shikha had no doubt in her mind that she had made the right choice. It was better than doing business management and joining a multinational. Private companies had only a profit motive. As a person with authority in the government scctor, you could do a lot of good without bothering too much about the cash register.

Shakuni was twenty-five now and she had a good job. Mrs Verma felt that it was time she got married. There was a new physical training instructor at the Seagull school.

Mathews was a retired army major. Mathews' father Philips was a politician and had been a member of parliament. Mathews was his only son. A good sportsman, Mathews had joined the National Defence Academy against his father's wishes. On passing out, he had joined the Guards regiment. As a major, he had captained the Guards football team. An injury sustained in a keenly fought football match had injured his knee. Despite surgery, he still limped. He was not fit for combat anymore. He was not interested in a desk job. He applied for, and got his release from the army.

His father Philips was still a member of the party's national advisory committee. The family-owned vast stretches of rubber estates in north Kerala. Mathews did not really have to work for a living. How ever his house was near the Sea Gull School. Mathews loved all sports and was good at most of them. It was the school's policy to finish the physical education periods before breakfast. So, the timing also suited him.

From seven to nine, he coached the girls in various sports including horse riding. After nine he was free to look into the business end of his family estates. After five, he would be back again with the girls, coaching the teams which would be participating in the inter schools contests.

Shakuni had been asked by Mrs. Varma to be around as a chaperone for the physical education classes. She also joined into the games with gusto. Shakuni was a strong girl with arms conditioned from her ferry woman days. She could soon play hockey better than most of the school girls. When the Sea Gulls hockey team went for their league matches to Trivandrum, both Mathews and Shakuni went with them. It was there that the camaraderie between the two of them blossomed into a full-fledged romance.

Shikha did well in her administrative services training. The course at the Dehra Dun centre had been an eye opener in many respects. Overall, it had been very enjoyable. Shikha had opted for a post in Kerala. Soon she was posted as a district magistrate in the Idukki district of north Kerala.

Shikha had by now lost all communication with her old flame, who had joined the police services. The boy had been posted to the Andaman Islands as the

Director of Transport. He was from Andhra Pradesh and his parents were after him to marry a wealthy girl. The dowry would be quite handsome, more than what he could ever hope to earn honestly as a police officer.

When Mathews and Shakuni returned with the team from Trivandrum, they went to Mrs Varma's office. She congratulated them all on their magnificent victory. After the students had left, Mathews and Shakuni stayed back. They told her that they wanted to get married. Mrs Varma was very happy for the couple. She suggested that Mathews ask for his parent's blessings. Mathews agreed.

Chapter 7   Shikha learns a Lesson

Shikha Varma did her job as district magistrate diligently. One of her many duties involved workers welfare projects in the rubber estates. She was also the head of the tribunal on labour affairs.

The plight of estate workers appalled her. The work was hard. There was no job security or health insurance. Worst of all, the children of estate workers had no access to education or health care. Their living conditions were pathetic. She had overheard estate owners say that they would oppose the setting up of schools for the labourer's children. If these children got educated, they would leave to the towns for easier jobs. There would be no one to work in the estates in the future.

Shikha thought that this logic was warped and that the mindset was archaic. You could not deny a generation an education, to deprive them of a choice. She set about drawing up a master plan for the uplift of the plantation worker community.

Mathews was pleasantly surprised when his father did not object too vehemently to his proposed nuptials with Shakuni. His mother was a trifle upset. She wanted him to marry into a good family.

Marriages in Kerala were more than a union between two souls. It was a business merger of two families. Mathew's parents had met Shakuni at school functions earlier and had been impressed by her vitality, character and poise. Philips considered himself to be a good judge of human ability. He was yet to come across someone who impressed him more than what Shakuni had. Beside he had a nebulous plan of a political future for the girl.

Shikha had her labour welfare document ready. She drew up a blueprint that would change the face of the plantations for ever. There would be a central settlement for the workers with a government run school and hospital. Buses would take the workers to their plantations and return with them in the evening. A crèche would be set up in the settlement for preschool children.

She proposed that the planters bear half the cost of the construction. The government would fund the other half. She called for a meeting with the plantation managers. The managers panicked. The estate owners were contacted. They decided that the initiative had to be scuttled at any cost.

The estate owners would work at a ministerial level to derail the proposals. The managers were asked to hire local leaders to oppose the plan. Shikha had no clue about the undercurrents.

The meeting started off on a pleasant note. Shikha congratulated them all on the previous year's production record. Then she got her secretary to read out the detailed proposal. Shikha was shocked when the first person to oppose her initiative was the labour union leader. He alleged that the plantation workers were being displaced from their current locations in a bid to capture their land. Slogans were shouted.

It was a capitalist nexus that had come up with this plan, said the union leader. He alleged that Shikha had received favours to put up this anti-labour proposal. Shikha was shocked. She would realize much later that the union leader had been bribed. The meeting and the proposal were abandoned. Shikha had been taken for a ride.

The wedding of Mathews and Shakuni was conducted with a lot of fanfare. It was attended by many political bigwigs from Delhi and Kerala. Newspapers ran whole pages on the story of Shakuni. They eulogized her travails and wrote about all that she had suffered. Shakuni had indeed surmounted horrendous odds. She had become a celebrity overnight.

 The first phase of Philips' plan was a roaring success. Shakuni had become a folk hero. Shikha was at the wedding. She and Shakuni were very close to each other. "Watch out for these plantation owners", Shikha warned her. They both laughed. They both knew that Philips was part of the plantation lobby that had made Shikha a laughing stock in the IAS community.

Shikha and Mathews hit it off very well. They shared many ideas and ideals. They got along so well that Shakuni tapped Mathews on the shoulder to tell him, "Hey, I am the bride- Remember? They all laughed heartily.

Shakuni and Mathews had a whirlwind honeymoon. They moved into Mathews' ancestral house with his parents. It was a sprawling demi-mansion and they had a host of servants. Shakuni and Mathews continued to work for the Sea Gull school. Philips now worked in an honorary capacity. Shakuni had however continued as the principal's secretary.

Mrs Varma was like a mother to her and she enjoyed being near her. Finally, Mrs Varma forced the decision upon Shakuni. The driver's daughter had finished her graduation and was looking for a job. If Shakuni could join the board of directors and resign her job, the girl could take the vacancy. The ploy was obvious. They both laughed and then cried a bit. Shakuni was finally leaving home.

Philips made sure that Shakuni accompanied him to all the political meetings. She was a hit at every occasion with her ready wit and warm smile. He soon had her elected as the women's convener of his party in Kerala. Mathews could see through Philips' plan now. Shakuni was a natural leader and Philips was grooming her for political leadership. Philips party had been out of power in the state for some time. A long-debated reservation policy for women in legislature had been passed. Thirty percent of the candidates for election had to be women. Shakuni was an obvious choice.

Shakuni was already a darling amongst the masses and she sailed through the elections with a thumping mandate. Philips party had a majority in the house and was invited to form the ministry. Shakuni was given a ministerial portfolio of plantations and agriculture.

One of the first things that Shakuni did in office was to get Shikha appointed as the plantation commission chairman. Shikha's blueprint for plantation workers was revived and soon became law. The plantation workers act was passed. The government met most of the expenses for infrastructure development in their settlements. Mathews worked closely with Shikha to monitor the progress of the act's implementation. The two of them toured the various plantations to supervise the project in Mathews' jeep.

The single largest plantation owner was Babu Ram. He was a multimillionaire who was reputed to have amassed his wealth through gold smuggling operations. He was now a powerful and respected business tycoon. He owned a chunk of the film industry and a couple of newspapers. He also owned a lion's share of the cardamom and tea plantations in the area. He had steadfastly resisted Shika's attempts to get the plantation act implemented in his estates.

Babu Ram had paid one of the workers to move court and obtain a stay order against shifting to the settlement. He also engineered a public interest litigation by an environmental agency against the creation of the settlement in its planned location. All work was put on hold as the matter was under the court's purview. This was a known ploy to stall any project. There would be hearings and adjournments. By the time the process of litigation was complete the project would not be viable with the available finances. While fresh financial sanctions were delayed, the ministry would change. The project would be dumped in the dustbin.

Chapter 10   Shikha at War

Shikha was not however going to give up without a fight. She enlisted Mathews' help. Together they investigated the environmentalist's concerns. The agency that had moved court for stalling the project was internationally recognized as an advocate for environmental issues. Shikha was sure that they had been misinformed about the rehabilitation plan. She had to make sure that they knew the truth. She sat with Mathews and prepared a blueprint. They captured on film, the dirt and squalor of the worker's dwellings. The final approved drawings of the proposed settlement were reproduced with captions. They consolidated evidence that the settlement would not adversely affect the ecology of the hills.

Mathews had in the meanwhile obtained a statement of the bank accounts of the environmental agency's local representative. A large deposit had been made into his account before the court appeal. He had received a payoff.

Armed with all these documents, one of Shikha's Foreign Service colleagues visited the agency's headquarters at Geneva. He presented the data to the chairman. Within a week, the case had been withdrawn and the local agent was out of a job. The labousrer who had appealed against shifting to the settlement also withdrew his case. An appeal was pleaded before the high court that Babu Ram was using stalling tactics to abort the welfare scheme for workers. The court passed an order that work should be commenced immediately.

Armed with a copy of this order Shikha and Mathews drew up at Babu Rams estate headquarters. Babu Ram seemed resigned to the inevitable. He claimed that he would start the work immediately. Acknowledging that he had been out-manoeuvred, he invited Mathews and Shikha to stay for dinner. Mathews politely refused. He knew Babu Ram's antecedents. He did not want them to get poisoned.

They left the estate headquarters with a sense of victory. They planned to drive down to Mathews' house. Shakuni would also join them later after a meeting with the visiting defence minister who was from Kerala.

The estate building was almost near the top of the mountain range. It was a long, winding and treacherous road down to the nearest town. Shikha realized that their jeep was going too fast. She was surprised. Mathews was always a careful driver. She turned to look at him. His face was pale and he was struggling with the gears. Someone had cut the brake line. The jeep could not be slowed. Half a kilometre ahead was a hairpin bend at the edge of the cliff. They would not be able to negotiate the curve at this speed. "Brace yourself", Mathews shouted as he tried to slow the jeep down by ramming the jeep into the rocky face on the right of the road.

Chapter 11   The Accident

He turned the steering wheel sharply to the right. The hairpin bend with its precipice ahead was two hundred meters ahead. Mathews' jeep careened off the rocks and hurtled towards the precipice balanced on two wheels. Shilpa would get crushed if the jeep tilted any further. Mathews grabbed Shilpa around her waist and pulled her across him. Using all his strength he hurled her over his side of the jeep and to the road.

She landed bruised, but unhurt. Then Mathews tried to jump. Before he could clear the jeep however the jeep had turned turtle and then it shot off the cliff. There was silence as it flew through the air. A plume of flame followed by an explosion pointed to the jeep's fiery end at the bottom of the gully. From his estate house window behind, Baburam saw the flash of flame. He raised his glass in a silent toast.

Mathews lay on the road, unmoving. Shilpa had seen the jeep go over the edge and thought for a moment that Mathews was still trapped in it. Then she saw him. Mathews was on the road at the curve lying motionless just meters away from the cliff's edge. Her heart leapt with joy. There was a moment's consternation. Why was he not moving? She scrambled to her feet. She was shaken but relatively unhurt by the fall. She ran to Mathews.

Mathews opened his eyes. He sensed Shikha leaning over him and calling his name. He opened his eyes. He had a vague idea of what had happened to him. He looked at Shikha. His eyes were full of calm. He told Shilpa. "I think my neck is broken. I cannot move my hands and legs".

 Shikha knew that she would have to keep all her wits about her. There was no time for tears now. She had to save his life. Shilpa realized that she would not be able to Shift Mathews on her own. She laid him out straight on the road, taking care not to move his neck. There was no traffic on this road. Unless someone from the estate had seen the crash and decided to investigate no vehicle would be coming that way. It was better to be safe. She rolled a few rocks on to the road on both sides of Mathews.

It was cold in the hills. There was nothing to cover Mathews with. She took off her coat and put it over his chest. Shikha had to call for help before it grew darker. She searched for her mobile. It had been thrown off when she fell to the road. Fortunately she found it. She rang up Shakuni and told her what had happened and gave their location. Her cell phone beeped once and went off. The battery had run out.

Shikha ran back to Mathews. He seemed to be sinking. He was not conscious any more. His breathing was shallow and he was turning blue around the lips. She lay down by his side holding his body close to warm him. Then she pried open his mouth and planting her lips carefully over his and started puffing air into his starved lungs. Slowly his colour came back.

In a while Mathews opened his eyes. "This is the way to die", he mumbled into her mouth. She gave a sigh of relief. "No" she told him, a warm joy flooding through her body. "This is the way to live".

Chapter 12   The Rescue

In took an hour for the Air Force helicopter to arrive. Shakuni had been with the defence minister when Shilpa's call came through. She told him what had happened. The minister immediately called the Air Chief on his mobile phone. It was not an easy task to rescue a man from the mountainside in the dark by helicopter. The Air chief passed his orders. Within minutes a search and rescue chopper was up in the air and heading for the hills.

It took them an hour to locate Matews and Shikha in the gathering dusk. The smouldering jeep had given them a clue to the location. Fortunately, the weather was good and there were no trees. The helicopter hovered over them, taking care to keep away from the cliffs face. A rope ladder was lowered. Four airmen climbed down to the mountain road and ran over to Mathews. A stretcher and equipment came next. The paramedics applied a collar around Mathews' neck and an oxygen mask to his face. The stretcher was winched into the helicopter. Shikha climbed the ladder next, keeping her eyes half closed and taking care not to look at the valley below. The rest of the men clambered in and the chopper was off.

When the helicopter reached Trivandrum, an ambulance was ready and waiting to whisk them away to a tertiary care neurological centre. An MRI image of Mathews' cervical spine confirmed their worst fears. His sixth cervical vertebra had fractured and dislocated. The bone edge had severed his spinal cord.

Mathews would never walk again. He would have no sensation or control over his legs or his body. Even his hands would be affected. The best he could expect was some movement at his shoulder and elbow. Mathews' movements and his ability to write too would be lost for ever and he would have no control over his bowel or his urine.

Mathews' life was still in danger. There was a real possibility that the swelling of his spinal cord and the ongoing injury cascades triggered within his body could temporarily at least affect his capacity to breathe. Meanwhile his neck was unstable. The collar provided only a minimum support. The doctors at the centre operated on him immediately. They put in a titanium plate to stabilize his neck to prevent further injury. The damage to the spinal cord was however irretrievable.

 Babu Ram's involvement in the accident could not be proven. There was little left of the jeep to provide any evidence of sabotage. The central bureau investigating team which raided his premises stumbled upon a startling finding. There was a large cache of sophisticated arms and ammunition. Babu Ram was arrested under the terrorist and disruptive activities act. The government took over the estate. The worker's settlement was built according to plan.

Mathews was in hospital for the next three months. Shakuni and Shikha took turns to be with him, caring for his every need. He understood the significance of what had happened. He would be paralyzed, a 'quadriparetic', for the rest of his life. He would need help, not only for mobility, but also to empty his bladder with a catheter or his bowels with enemas. There would invariably be problems with skin breakdowns and urinary infections.

Chest infections killed many spinal cord injury victims. Breathing was controlled through two sets of nerves. The phrenic nerve which controlled his diaphragm was the main force drawing air into his lungs. As this nerve exited the spinal cord at the level of the third cervical vertebra it was uninjured in Mathews' case. How-ever there was another set of nerves which provided some force to breathing, especially in forcefully breathing out. These were the intercostal nerves coming out of the spinal cord at the thoracic level. There were twelve pairs of intercostal nerves, one at each level of the thoracic vertebrae. These nerves were no longer under volitional control if the spinal cord was damaged in the neck. They would develop some respiratory equilibrium of their own later. There was a however a tendency for phlegm to collect in the lungs, which could result in pneumonia.

Another major cause of concern for the rest of his life would be his urinary system. In the earlier days, most of the patients who survived a spinal cord injury would die of urinary infection. Today there was a better understanding of how to manage the urinary tract. A clean catheter would have to be passed into the bladder intermittently to drain out the urine. Even with the best of care however, urinary tract infections would occur. They would periodically need to get the urine cultured to check for growth of dangerous bacteria. Urinary tract infections would need to be treated in time to prevent damage to the kidneys.

The care of his skin would be another challenge. As the skin of his back and buttocks was senseless. Lacking the invariable protective movements to prevent skin damage over bony prominences skin would breakdown. These ulcers over pressure points could occur when he lay immobile in bed or even more when he sat up. This would cause the so-called pressure or bed sores. Once these occurred, these would be difficult to treat. Some of these ulcers needed plastic surgery for closure. Despite all the care at hospital, with two hourly turning and using soft padding, Mathew's had developed an ulcer over his sacrum. Fortunately, it healed without further operations.

There were a myriad other problems that he would have to look out for. Clots could form in his legs as the flabby muscles would not push the blood back to the heart. His blood pressure could shoot up, even producing strokes in some people. There is so much that we take for granted in daily life would pose a challenge to a para or quadriplegic individual. The only positive note was that his brain was intact and his intellect normal. After an inevitable, early phase of depression, his attitude turned more positive. He would do the best he could, with his life.

The girls scoured the internet for anyone who could give them some hope. There is a whole industry which survives on selling false hopes to the hopeless. The surgeons at the institute had warned them to watch out for charlatans. There were many who promised miracle cures for injured spinal cords. They wasted the precious time and money of unfortunate victims. These poor people could use their resources better, for rehabilitation and resettlement. Shakuni and Shikha knew that they would have to whet each hope with scientific logic before discussing it with Mathews.

Spinal cord injuries often affected young people at the peak of their lives. There had been many articles regarding the use of stem cell therapies for spinal cord injured patients. This was based on the discovery in the last decade of neural stem cells. These were cells inside and even outside the nervous system, which could multiply and differentiate into functioning nerve cells. This discovery threw out the age-old assertion that nerve cells, once lost, could not be replaced. This discovery was giving new hope to patients with a wide variety of neural disorders.

All over the third world, there were people experimenting on spinal cord injury patients, injecting known sources of stem cells into or near injured cords. Shakuni and Shikha had a long discussion with a neurosurgical friend, on its benefits. He had discouraged them from pursuing this course.

Firstly, the devastating paralysis associated with a cut or crushed spinal cord was mainly due to breaks in the long nerve processes or tracts which passed through the cord. The nerve cells themselves, which controlled movement were either in the brain or at their separate levels in the cord. Injecting cells, which could evolve into neurons was not very rationa. In the more advanced countries, the controls on human trials were more stringent. There were few human trials on stem cell implantation in spinal cord injured patients. The girls decided not to pursue that avenue.

It was Shakuni who brought the magazine article to Shikha's notice. It was an interview with an Indian scientist who was working on a program called the brain machine interface. Shikha immediately recognized the man.

Rajeev had been her senior at the Indian Institute of Technology. He had been, in Shikha's words, "A drab chap with big spectacles who always came first in class". Shikha went through the details of his work on the internet. The concept of converting the brain's synaptic signals into electrical waves and using these impulses to activate muscles beyond an area of nerve injury was not new. The earlier machines however were cumbersome and could not be practically used by patients.

Chapter 15   Rajeev

 Brain machine interphases collected impulses generated by neurons of the cerebral cortex. These impulses would be amplified and used to operate a machine. For a spinal cord injury patient to walk, brain impulses would need to be channelled back to the spinal cord below the level of injury. Brain function is incredibly complex. Movements or functions are planned, initiated, coordinated, fine-tuned and controlled by connections between multiple regions. Finalised movement plans moved down the spinal cord to individual final control centres at each level of the cord. These movement plans had to bypass the injured zone and be reintroduced in the intact distal cord for meaningful recovery.

Rajeev had recently developed an implantable brain machine interface device. The aim was to reconnect the spinal cord whose long fibre tracts had been disrupted. The device would collect signals from the spinal cord above the injury and transmit those signals across to each level of the spinal cord. It was an ambitious program. They would be rewiring the injured spinal cord. Implantable microprocessors were making this possible. They had shown success in some monkey experiments and were planning to go ahead with human trials soon.

 Shikha got in touch with Rajeev. She sent him the details of Mathews' case and wondered if he could help. She got a reply within a week. Rajeev remembered Shikha fondly from the institute days. He had got the necessary sanctions from the university. Mathews' case would be an ideal one to try the device on. His injury was just three months old. If the rewiring was successful, his nerves and muscles could start to work again, under his volition.

Rajeev had another suggestion. Would Shikha join him to help him with the program? She would have the advantage of knowing Mathews well, in addition to being a computer scientist. Mathews would have to be at the institute for about six months for the implantation and muscle nerve re-education to be successful.

Rajeev cautioned her that the results were unpredictable. All the effort could lead up a dead alley. He also hoped that Shikha had not forgotten all her computer science. Shikha had to smile to herself. Some people never changed. They had a long discussion. Shakuni could not leave the country for six months. Besides Philips needed her help now to run his affairs. He had been recently diagnosed to have Alzheimer's disease and tended to forget things.

Shika had been considering quitting the administrative services for some time. She would love to get back to her computer science work. She would fly down with Mathews to Rajeev's institute in the United States. They flew down to the centre.

The institute had a well-equipped spinal injury unit where Mathews would stay. The technology and assistance here, at the patient's disposal, was more schematised than what was available in India. He was given a computer console with the controls strapped to his palm. With this he could sit up in bed, summon his wheelchair and even get his breakfast. With all this gadgetry, he could maximize the things he could do.

Mathews often wished that his injury were one level lower in the cervical spine. He would then have had at least partial use of his fingers. Now he had to operate his palmtop controls with his chin. There was an also an intensive physiotherapy and electrical stimulation program. This would keep his muscles and nerves active and prevent them from degenerating before rewiring could be attempted.

Shikha plunged into her new role as research assistant with gusto. She would be in the laboratory early in the morning and it would be late in the night when she and Rajeev would decide to call it a day. Irrespective of the time, she would spend some time with Mathews, briefing him on the day's work to keep his spirits up.

Chapter 15   The Finale

Finally, the spinal cord electrical interface was implanted. With the best of skills and care only around 30% of fibre reconnections was perfect in alignment. The rest would be retrained. Re-education of muscles commenced. Mathews had practiced with a simulator in the lab. He would try to move a joint and then press the button for an electrical impulse to elicit a muscle contraction.

 With the interface implanted, he did not have any buttons to press. He had to generate the thought impulse. That took training. It was hard on Mathews. He had to relearn movements. He remembered the poem he had learned in childhood about the centipede learning to walk. It collapsed trying to figure out as to which leg came after which. Mathews thought that his problem was infinitely more complex than the centipedes'. Every human movement was infinitely more complex that the insects crawl.

The intensity of the electric current had to be programmed. Mathews could only elicit feeble and ineffective contractions now. Over a period of time as he gained confidence and control, useful movement could be aimed for. Shakuni visited the institute whenever she could. Political affairs in

Kerala were always in turmoil and one had to ride the roller coaster with care. Eight months were over before the team decided that Mathews could be flown back to India, where his retraining could continue.

Shakuni waited in the VIP lounge of the international airport for Mathews' flight. Philips condition had worsened and he was not capable of looking after himself outside his home. He and his wife would wait for them at home. Shakuni looked out over the tarmac. The flight was landing.

There was Mathews in his wheel chair. He looked happy to be back. Behind him were Shikha and Rajeev. The wheel chair stopped in the passenger's zone. Slowly, before Shakuni's tearful eyes Mathews got up from the wheel chair and walked the few steps into her arms. Shakuni burst into tears.

Shikha and Rajeev helped Mathews to a chair. Shikha turned to Shakuni. After a tearful embrace, Shikha introduced Rajeev to her. "Now that I have got your husband back, I decided to get one for myself too. Meet Rajeev. We got married yesterday".

Sushila

Chapter 1   *Ramachandran*

Sushila's birth was an occasion of great joy. There were two sets of grandparents to spice up the celebrations. Her father Ramachandran had been in the Air Force until recently. Five years ago, a tragic accident on the highway had cost him his family. Ramachandran had survived.

Ramachandran's wife and two daughters had been the focus of his life. For two years, he had drifted, aimless. Fortunately, the structured discipline of the uniformed services had kept him sane. He slowly clawed back into life. In the next three years, he got himself his graduation and a diploma in business management. After fifteen years in the Forces, Ramachandran, or Ram as his friends called him accepted retirement.

His parents were old and his only sister was settled abroad. He would settle in Kerala. It was his destiny to look after his parents, he thought. He assumed that all that had happened was the insurmountable course of Karma.

Ram was still in his early thirties when he retired from the Air Force. He got himself a job as a marketing executive for a group of property developers. The job was well paid and the organizational skills he had developed in his air force career helped. He was quite successful at his work. Life was settling into a fixed groove. Ram was therefore taken aback one day, when his uncle button holed him with a marriage proposal.

Sujatha was the daughter of a friend of his uncle. The family had been settled in the Middle East for several years. The girl had been educated there and had later worked as a teacher at the Indian school. They had recently returned to India. Sujatha was old by Kerala standards. She was twenty-eight, well beyond the comfort zone of arranged marriages. Ram's uncle was very persuasive and his arguments sound.

Ram was now thirty-five years old. He could start afresh and raise another family. His parents wanted grandchildren. In this alliance everything was working out well. His uncle was persistent. Ram had not seriously considered remarriage. He knew that he could never forget the time he had spent with his first family.

Ram was hesitant. His parents were very keen that he should marry again. There was no heir for the property and his sister was showing no inclination to ever return to India. Finally, he relented. He agreed to meet Sujatha in her house.

It was the custom during wedding negotiations in Kerala. The boy with his parents would visit the girl's house. There would be refreshments served and pleasantries exchanged. If matters proceeded on course, the parents would leave the boy and girl alone in the living room. This was the opportunity for the young people to talk freely and to gauge each other for compatibility. This was the only semblance of interaction of a prospective couple that conservative society allowed. Dating was obviously taboo. "I have been through this before", Ramachandran reminisced with a bit of anguish.

Chapter 2   The Wedding

Sujatha herself had served the tea. She was a charming girl, very polished. She reminded Ram of some of the young flyer's wives he had seen in his Air Force days. Those girls had looked sexy, yet seemed capable of taking on the world. Sujatha could have easily passed as one of them. She spoke confidently and carried herself with poise. Tea was soon over and the parents retired.

Ram started the conversation. He told her quickly about himself. He told her about his earlier marriage and the happy family life that they had shared. There was a crack in his voice and a tear in his eye as he recounted the horrible car accident, where he had been the lone survivor. He liked Sujatha and if she were willing to accept him with his memories, he could ask the parents to go ahead with the arrangements.

He looked up. To his surprise, Sujatha was crying. Tears were rolling down her cheeks. She had been so moved by his story that she could not control her emotions. Ram had to hold himself back from putting his arm around her to comfort her. Such intimacy would not be acceptable before marriage.

Not in Kerala and definitely not in her parent's living room.

They sat for a while in silence. They would have to call their parents in now. "Is it 'Yes' or 'No'?" he asked her. She nodded an emphatic yes. He offered her his handkerchief, which she kept, pressed to her face for a long time. She wiped her tears, but would not return the hanky. They smiled at each other.

Ram realized with a shock that they were already falling in love. The wedding was a simple affair. Only a few close relatives were invited. Ram had been against the idea of a honeymoon. Sujatha's father had however made the arrangements. He had booked a cruise for them on a luxury vessel sailing to the Far East. This would ensure ten days of togetherness, away from the rest of the world.

The cruise was heavenly. Ram realized the worth of his father in law's wisdom. These seven days would forge them a bond that would last a lifetime. A new life had begun for both of them.

They stayed at Ram's house with his parents. Sujatha's parents lived just a couple of kilometres away. Ram's work involved a lot of traveling. Sujatha stayed at home. She was busy getting pampered as the favourite daughter of two houses. She considered taking up a job herself, but decided against it. Sujatha realized that she was getting on in years and should complete her family as soon as possible.

Chapter 3   Sushila

A year went by. Sujatha was expecting her first baby. For her first confinement, Sujatha was admitted to the local mission hospital. True, there were better equipped hospitals in town, but this place was just a furlong from Sujatha's house. It would be convenient for them all. The hospital had a gynaecologist. The premises were neat and the nurses courteous.

It was a far cry from what Ram had experienced when his first child from earlier marriage was born at a busy military hospital. There, no one had had time to talk to them. His wife's delivery had been relatively uneventful. There was a lady from Bihar in an adjacent cot who had created a huge uproar in the ward. After a difficult delivery, someone had told her that her baby was a boy.

When they brought the baby to her from the resuscitation unit, she had been horrified to notice that it was a girl. She had refused to accept the baby or to feed it. They had to subject the baby to genetic testing at a national centre. Here, it was confirmed that the baby was indeed theirs. "It all depends on the culture ethos of the place", thought Ram. In Kerala, a girl child was thought to be no less auspicious.

Sujatha's labour pains were not progressing as expected. The doctor decided on a caesarean section. The operation theatre had to be opened and fumigated. The anaesthesiologist had to be called. The power supply had tripped. The watchman with the keys to the generator room had disappeared. He was finally traced to a toddy shop.

Finally, everything went off well. The baby was a little blue when she was born. After a couple of hard whacks on the butt from the scrub nurse, she started to wail. Sujatha and her baby were kept in the intensive care unit for a day. A day later, she and the baby were home. They named their daughter Sushila.

Sushila was a pampered infant. The two sets of grandparents took turns at spoiling her. After her baby grew up a bit, she would take up a job, thought Sujatha. It was toxic to stay at home and spend the whole day cooking and cleaning. It did something to your psyche. The simplest thing was to get a job as a teacher.

It was not easy to get a school teachers job in Kerala. You needed political connections and had to pay a heavy bribe to get a job in a government owned school. Private schools were better and the children there were better behaved. The salaries you received were however, pathetic.

School teachers and nurses were amongst the most poorly paid people in Kerala. Sujatha thought that a monthly salary of four thousand rupees was insulting.

The government had fixed salaries for school teachers. The Various charitable institutions which owned and managed these educational institutions managed to keep most of the money, paying the staff only a pittance. As you were made to sign for the full amount dictated by the government, you ended up paying tax for the money that was going into the management's coffers. There was no option. If you did not like it, there were a thousand other aspirants for the post.

There were plenty of new fields opening up, especially in the information technology sector. Most of these jobs would involve a lot of commuting. Sujatha thought that she could decide on a job later. If she had not got married, she would have joined a multinational company and worked her way up. With a family, one had to compromise.

Chapter 4

Sushila has a Seizure

 Ramakrishnan was happy with the work he was doing. Unlike in government service, in the private sector the emphasis was on productivity. Individual egos were not as fragile. If a man did a good job, he was appreciated and potentially rewarded. Ram felt that there was no resentment to his success. People in his organization did not feel threatened when he clinched a few more deals or got letters of appreciation from his clients.

Ram was honest in his dealings with his customers and tried to offer them the most appropriate deals. He could guide his clients on the nuances of procuring bank loans and on the hidden nuances of interest rates. Even after he sold off a flat, he would help in organizing repair jobs and advice on and assist in necessary engineering efforts and house modifications. Innate sincerity is far superior to cultivated communication skills. His empathy and compassion were appreciated by his clients. The clients swore by him. His company started to consider him a valuable employee.

When Sushila's second birthday was being celebrated her mother was expecting her next baby.

The second child too was a girl. They called her Kumkum. Sushila was very excited at the prospect of having a little sister to look after. With four grandparents around, Sushila never lacked attention. The new entrant, Kumkum, was a plumper version of Sushila.

Sushila was three years old, when she had her first seizure. She had been running around with a blocked nose and swollen tonsils for a week. It was only when her temperature crossed 100 degree Fahrenheit, that she could be confined to bed, with a threat of injections and hospital if she did not rest. Ramachandran was on tour and Kumkum was with Sujatha's mother.

Sujatha sat by her sick daughter's side, reading a book. She had taken Sushila to the pediatrician in the morning. The lady doctor had started her on a course of antibiotics and paracetamol. The girl had an upper respiratory infection. Too many ice creams and cold drinks, was the doctor's verdict. It was true, mused Sujatha. The refrigerator was always stocked and Sushila's grandparents were over-indulgent.

It was two in the afternoon and Sujatha had had her lunch. She lay down next to Sushila and closed her eyes. A sudden cry from Sushila woke her up. The girl's eyes had rolled up and she was having a series of spasms. She was unconscious.

Sujatha screamed. Her parents came running up. The driver was summoned. They rushed with the little girl to hospital. The fits stopped before they reached the hospital and Sushila had fallen asleep. They admitted the child with the mother in hospital. The nurses brought her fever down with cold sponges and started her on medication. In a day she was all right. They decided against doing a CT scan of the head. The child was well, why expose her to radiation? Sushila had a tendency to febrile fits. If the parents were careful and made sure that they treated any fevers immediately, no more fits would occur. She would grow out of this trait when she was five to eight years old.

Chapter 5   Sushila joins School

 Sushila had no more febrile fits after her first attack. They followed the doctor's advice to the dot. The moment Sushila developed a hint of fever, her mother and grandparents would rush her to hospital. There they would sponge her and keep her temperature down till the fever resolved.

Sushila joined nursery school when she was four years old. The trouble started when Sushila was five years old and in class 1. One day, her teacher called Sujatha over for a little chat. She wanted to know if all was well at home. Sushila was not coping well at school. She was a slow student. She passed urine in her clothes and would sometimes sit, staring blankly ahead. Her teacher felt that it was a sign of stress.

Sujatha did not tell anyone else about what the teacher had told her. But she took special efforts to ensure that the girl did not feel neglected in any way.

One night, the whole family was having dinner when it happened. Ram noticed that Sushila was not eating her food. She stared blankly ahead and seemed to be munching, but her mouth was empty and the food in her plate was untouched. Ram called to her, but she would not respond. Then, suddenly she snapped out of it. She started eating again. Ram was furious. He shouted at her. "What do you think you are doing?" Sushila looked confused. She could only say, "Something was smelling very funny".

There was a psychiatrist in the military hospital at Kochi. Ram decided to take his daughter there for a check up. When they went to Kochi however, he was disappointed. The psychiatrist was on leave. The doctor who attended to them listened to the story. He checked the little girl's temperature and peered down her throat. He then prescribed some vitamins and counseled the child. Ram returned home reassured.

However the staring spells in class continued. The teacher would ignore them. The girl had been checked up by a doctor. She would probably grow out of it. Sushila continued to do badly in class. She was shy and sometimes resentful of her sister. Even with all the coaching that Sujatha was giving her, she was just scraping through her class examinations. Sujatha was certain that there was something wrong with her daughter. On quite a few occasions she had noticed that Sushila's clothes smelt of urine. Ramachandran felt that the girl was just spoilt. Be firm with her, he told his wife. Don't let her think that she can get away with it. Sujatha tried being firm. Sushila became even more withdrawn and uncommunicative. Sujatha wanted to take her to the Psychiatrist. The rest of the family was against it. To get a label of Psychiatric illness could be fatal for the girl's matrimonial prospects in the future. It did not matter if she did not do well at school. They were well off and had enough property. They would certainly be able to find a good husband for their daughter when she grew up.

When Sushila was in class three, Kumkum also joined the school. They were a study in contrasts. While Sushila always scraped through her examinations, Kumkum was always first in class. Where Sushila was withdrawn and reticent, Kumkum was vivacious and confident. The teachers could hardly believe that they were both sisters. When guests came home, it was Kumkum who entertained them and charmed them with her wit. Sushila would hide behind the door. "At least, she has stopped wetting her clothes" thought Sujatha. Sushila had not. She had started using the school toilet to rinse out her urine soaked clothes.

She scraped through her class three examinations only because there was a government ruling that no child would be failed in the primary classes. One day, when Sushila was in class four, Sujatha got an urgent call from the school. Sushila was very sick and needed to be taken to hospital immediately. By the time Sujatha and her father reached the school the girl had already been shifted to the hospital. The headmistress told them what happened.

Sushila had fallen unconscious in class. According to the class teacher, she had stopped breathing and had turned blue. She started breathing only after the teacher had laid her out flat and thumped her hard on the chest. The school headmistress had called for an ambulance and shifted her to the government hospital.

When Sujatha and her father reached the hospital, Sushila was in the intensive care unit. A tube had been passed through her throat and she was hooked on to a ventilator. She had been having continuous seizures, the duty doctor explained. They had to put her on a ventilator and give her drugs to paralyze her before they managed to stop the attack. Even now when the drugs wore off, she was having fits. The doctors planned to keep her on the ventilator till the fits were controlled.

The senior neurologist interviewed the parents in the evening. "Had she had any problems earlier"? He asked the parents. Sujatha told him about her staring spells, the urine stained clothes and her dismal school performance. The neurologist was furious. The poor girl had been having seizures for so long and not received treatment. It was but natural that her school performance was abysmal and her social graces poor. He started giving her anti-seizure medicines through a feeding tube.

Over the next week, Sushila recovered. She was off the ventilator and asking for dosas and idlis soon. She was on two medicines to prevent fits. An MRI scan had been done soon after her admission into hospital. It was reported as normal. At the end of seven days Sushila returned home with her parents. The neurologist had called her for a follow up examination after a month.

The school refused to take her back. The attack had been alarming. If the girl had died in class, the school would have been blamed. "Sushila was such a poor student anyway and now she had developed epilepsy. Her being in school would be bad for the other children. Besides, who would accept the responsibility if she developed another fit in school and died?"

Ram tried to reason with them. He got a letter from the neurologist that Sushila was under treatment now and unlikely to develop a full blown fit. Minor seizures might occur but they would not be life threatening. The headmistress was adamant and she refused to budge. As the interview progressed she got irritated and turned a shade nasty. She suggested that if Ramachandran started causing any trouble for them even Kumkum would be asked to leave the school.

Ram was furious. He contacted a lawyer. The Lawyer shot off a legal notice to the school. Discriminating against a child with epilepsy could be challenged in a court of law. The school authorities also sought legal advice. Finally the governing board called Ramachandran to the school. They suggested a compromise. Kumkum of course would continue in the school. In fact they had recommended her for a scholarship. They would let Sushila continue in the school rolls, on condition that she would not attend class, but only come for the examinations and that too accompanied by her mother.

This would be good for Sushila, they reasoned. The present government policy was not to fail anyone till class eight. So the girl would have, on record, attended school till class eight from the safety of her home. Sujatha could teach Sushila the class portions. If she faced any difficulty, private tutors could be arranged. Ram left, saying that he would have to discuss the matter with his wife.

Sujatha was happy to take on the responsibility of her daughters education. She had a deep sense of guilt at having delayed her daughter's treatment and wanted to do something extra. This would be her opportunity. They agreed to the school body's proposal.

Sushila's fits were now under reasonable control. She was a changed girl now. Earlier she had a sense of being a failure and an embarrassment at school. The anguish at causing her parents disappointment had made her a recluse. Now when she had fallen sick, the whole family had rallied around her. Surely they loved her. Her mother would help her with school work. Together they would show the teachers that there were two bright girls in the family, not one.

Now that she was on medication, she did not wet her clothes any more. Her self confidence improved. Sushila's class teacher had been sure that she would fail her final examination. When the test results came in, she was shocked. Sushila had passed and passed well. She told the headmistress that the girl's progress had been extraordinary. Maybe they could consider allowing her back into regular class.

The headmistress had a discussion with the management. Then she called Sujatha for an interview. After general enquiries about her daughter's well being, she came to the point. If Sujatha were willing to join the school as a teacher, they could let Sushila attend regular classes. With her mother in school, the authorities would be less worried about any seizure the girl might have.

Chapter 8   An Operation is Planned

Sushila had not had any major seizures since her hospital admission. However some minor fits continued to occur. Sushila would know when a fit was coming. She would sit in a corner before her mind went blank for a while. Sometimes there would be a feeling of dread or a funny smell. Mostly, others who did not know her would not realize that a fit had occurred. On a couple of occasions however her left hand had jerked spasmodically before she passed out.

Her parents took Sushila back to the neurologist for a review. He had not reduced the doses of drugs as some seizures were still persisting. Sushila's outlook to her sickness had changed remarkably. She understood the nature of her illness and knew that there were some precautions to be taken. To compensate for her disability she put in an extra effort into her studies. She was coming in the first five in class regularly. By the time she reached class eight, she had firmly resolved to become a doctor.

The neurologist had another MRI examination of Sushila's brain. He diagnosed Sushila to have a condition he called hippocampal sclerosis. Surgical removal of this seizure focus could cure her condition. He suggested that they contact a neurosurgeon who specialized in this type of surgery.

Ram was taken aback. He had no intention of subjecting his daughter to a brain operation. A friend of his from Madras had told him of a doctor there, who could cure epilepsy permanently with medicines alone. The school had closed for summer vacations. So, leaving Kumkum under the care of her grand parents the family moved to Madras. The doctor in the posh private clinic evaluated Sushila.

He was a smooth talker and very effusive in his expression of concern. He went through all the old reports and rubbished the idea of surgery. Then he changed the medicines that Sushila's neurologist had given her. They could go back home now, he said. In a month, he would see her again and by this time he was sure that the medication requirements would have decreased. In three months he would stop the medicines.

Ram was very happy. True, the clinic had been expensive, but this is what he had hoped for, cure without surgery. They returned by train to Kerala. They had scarcely unpacked when her seizures started again. This time they were full blown fits and they came one after the other without Sushila becoming conscious. They rushed her back to the government hospital.

Fortunately the neurologist who had treated Sushila earlier was there when they reached the hospital. This time, they could control the fits without putting her on the ventilator. After the crisis was over, a contrite Sujata told the neurologist all that had happened. He was a bit upset. But he had heard of the Madras clinic before. He turned away muttering "Charlatans".

The older medications were restarted. The school was still closed. He suggested that they attend the epilepsy surgery centre he recommended. The centre had a waiting list and it was worth registering with them as early as possible. After their fiasco at Madras, Ram had been suitably chastened. What was the most surprising however was Sujatha's attitude. She was very keen to undergo the operation and full of optimism about its outcome.

Sushila was so enthusiastic about her operation that the neurologist got worried. He had to caution her that there were risks involved in the operation and that she might still need to continue her anti seizure medication. Somehow it was difficult to dampen her enthusiasm.

At the epilepsy center Sushila was evaluated by a team of doctors including neurologists and neurosurgeons. An MRI and an EEG were repeated and then she underwent a test called a video EEG. Sushila was kept in a room which was monitored by a closed circuit TV system. Her mother was with her. EEG electrodes had been connected to her scalp and anti seizure medicines had been withdrawn the previous day. When a seizure started her mother would press a button which would start both video and EEG recordings. A nurse would rush in to help and give injections if the seizure was continuing.

Sushila threw a fit the same evening. Suddenly her face had gone blank. Sujatha ran to press the button. Sushila's left arm and leg were jerking uncontrollably and her head had turned away to one side. The nurse administered an injection in the girls vein. Sushila's taut body relaxed and she drifted off to sleep.

The doctors sat and analyzed the fit and the other reports. They then called in the parents. One of the young doctors projected the MRI scan on to a screen. He identified the hippocampus for them in the medial part of the temporal lobes. He then showed them that the right hippocampus looked smaller than the other. They were then shown the EEG record which showed abnormal looking spike discharges in two strips. This also corresponded to the right temporal lobe.

The team then discussed the treatment plan. They would remove the right amygdala and the hippocampus along with four centimeters of the temporal lobe. The hippocampus and its connections were involved in memory and emotions. With long standing fits however the memory storage function would have been, at least partially be taken over by the opposite hippocampus. If the operation were being planned on the left side, speech would have been a concern. All right handed people and most left handed people had their speech control center on the left.

By removing this focus of abnormal electrical discharges they hoped that her seizures would become easier to control, if not disappear. The earlier a person who had seizures underwent operation, the better were the chances of achieving good control.

Sushila was given an appointment for surgery during her Christmas vacation.

They returned home. Sushila was at her best. She excelled in everything that she did. She represented her school and later the state in the national 'spell bee' competition.

Sushila would tell everyone of the operation she would undergo in December. For her it seemed to be an exciting holiday plan. Soon it was December.

Chapter 10   The Operation

Sushila and Sujatha were admitted in the pre operative ward. A patch of hair over Sujatha's right ear had been shaved and her hair thoroughly rinsed with a shampoo. She was wheeled into the operating suite at seven in the morning. Sujatha was anxious, but her daughter reassured her. Inside the theatre, the walls gleamed. There were monitors and a large anesthesia machine with knobs for controlling gas flows. There were lamps on the ceiling and a central table with sophisticated controls. This was the OT table and she would be lying on it for the surgery.

An anesthesiologist had injected a milky white fluid called Propofol into Sushila's vein. She drifted off to sleep. A tube was placed in her throat which was connected to the anesthesia machine. The machine would be breathing for her. Everything including her rate and depth of breathing and the gases she inhaled would be controlled by the machine. There was a needle in her radial artery to measure her blood pressure, a catheter in her bladder to measure her urine flow and a probe in her nose to measure her body temperature.

The scrub nurse was ready with three different trolleys containing a variety of strong and fine surgical instruments. The designs of some of these instruments were unchanged since prehistoric times. There were also electromedical equipments like the cautery instrument which would help the surgeon to control bleeding by coagulating blood vessels. A gold colored pneumatic drill would help them to saw through the skull bone. The neurologist's assistant had got an EEG machine ready. Sterile strips of electrodes were lying on the scrub nurses trolley. These would be kept on the brain surface during the operation to check for abnormally discharging areas. These areas would need removal if the seizures were to be controlled.

The surgeons took over now. The head was fixed firmly with clamp. There should be no unexpected movement during the operation. A line of blood appeared on Sushila's scalp as a neat curving cut was made above the right ear. The scalp was peeled from the underlying muscle and the edges clipped to prevent bleeding. The muscle was then lifted off the bone using the cautery. The drill was then brought in. There was a roar as a burr rotating at more than fifty thousand rounds per minute drilled a hole in her skull bone. The burr was now changed for an oscillating saw, which had a 'foot plate' to protect the dura mater, the underlying firm membranous covering of the brain. With the saw the surgeon cut a neat semi circle of bone and handed over to the scrub nurse. She in turn packed it away, safely wrapped in a moistened pad. The dura mater was now cut. This was the tough protective layer of the meninges that enveloped the brain. The electrodes were now on the brain surface and the abnormal areas mapped. An operating microscope was now wheeled in.

The surgeon was slower now using the fine tipped instruments with delicate virtuosity as he removes the white matter of the temporal lobe of the brain. He drew a small gush of fluid from the temporal horn of the lateral ventricle of the brain. This was what he had been waiting for. Along the medial wall of the temporal horn lay the hippocampus and the amygdala, two structures that he would remove, before removing the rest of the anterior temporal lobe. The surgery was complete. The electrodes were replaced to check for any residual seizure activity. It was time for hemostasis and closure.

Chapter 11   The Recovery

When Sushila woke up, she was already in the intensive care unit. There was a constant and persistent beeping noise. It took her a while to realize that it was the sound of her own heart beat, being monitored on an instrument panel overhead. There was a dull pain in her head and her throat was feeling parched and sore. She put her hand up and felt a bandage.

A nurse had come up on seeing her move. "I want to pass urine, I am thirsty and my head hurts", she complained to the nurse. "There is a tube inside your bladder, which is giving you a sensation of wanting to pass urine and it is better that you don't drink anything now". The nurse was reassuring her. They gave her an injection, into her IV line and she drifted off to sleep again. The next morning she woke up bright and early.

Sushila was feeling much better now. There was still a little headache, but her urine catheter was out. A probationer nurse came over and helped her to brush her teeth. Then the nurse gave her a glass of juice to drink. Soon the doctors came for their rounds. There never seemed to be a moment's pause in the unit.

Sushila would be shifted to the ward soon. Here she could be with her mother. In another three days she could go home .She might have to miss the first two weeks of school. The surgeon warned her that she would have to continue her antiepileptic drugs for six more months.

Sushila was back to school in another two weeks. The staring spells or absences that she had been having no longer troubled her. She was preparing for her national scholarship examinations now. Her parents were happy that she had come out of surgery without any problems. They had been warned about the possibility of memory loss. To them it seemed that Sushila was absolutely fine.

Sushila was aware that there were some changes. She was having some problem with mathematics and her store of words was not what it had been. She knew that her proficiency in solving complex mathematical problems had gone down. She had been expected to win the science scholarship but she did not. She also lost in the preliminary rounds of the 'spell bee'. She stopped her music classes, she no longer appreciated the nuances of the notes. Sushila knew that some facets of herself had changed. To the rest of them she appeared the same. She was still the same pleasing personality and her school performance remained excellent.

Her desire to pursue a career in medicine had been reinforced by her experience as a patient. In a year's time, she would start her medical entrance preparations in earnest. Kumkum and Sushila were very close to each other now. They studied together and shared the same clothes and story books. Kumkum was sure that she wanted to try for admissions to the IIT's after she finished her twelfth.

Soon it was time for Sushila's tenth board examinations. She was still on some medication. The neurologist had reviewed her and decided against stopping her drugs. There were still a few abnormalities on her EEG. Sushila seemed disappointed. Finally he stopped one of her medicines and let the other continue. Sushila was tolerating the drug well and doing well at school. He did not want to let her run the risk of having seizures again.

Chapter 12   A Holiday

Sushila secured very good marks in her tenth. She had opted for the biology group for her eleventh and her twelfth. Ram had been keen that she should study mathematics too. Once you dropped mathematics your career options were restricted. Sushila was however hell bent on becoming a doctor and she had lost her love of math. Sujatha supported her daughter's decision. The girl was mature enough to make her own choices.

In the holidays after her tenth the family went on a holiday to Singapore. Ram and the girls had applied for their passports only in February. Sujatha already had hers. Fortunately, a scheme had been introduced by the government called the Tatkal scheme. If you paid two thousand rupees extra with your application, you could get your passport within a month. But police verifications still had to be gone through.

Ram had booked their tickets for the fifteenth of April. They received their passports on the thirteenth. It had been touch and go.

They had taken an international flight from Madras at the unearthly hour of two in the morning. Within four hours, they were at Singapore. The airport itself was a marvelous engineering masterpiece. The city of Singapore was built like any advanced city in the west and the people were hospitable.

Five days whirled past. They had boat rides in the moonlight and a day at the amusement park. There was sightseeing and there was a lot of shopping. It was the experience of a lifetime. Their last night in Singapore they were to witness a fireworks display. The dazzling display went on late into the night. They were all exhausted. It was nearing midnight when Sushila told her parents that she had had enough.

Sushila and her mother went back to their hotel room. Ramachandran and Kumkum would sit through to the end of the festivities. Sushila had not taken her medicines that evening. Sujatha was rummaging through the bag for them when she heard her daughter cry out. Sushila was having a seizure. In a few minutes the spasmodic movements ceased and the girl became unconscious.

Sujatha called the hotel reception for help. By the time the ambulance arrived, Sushila had woken up. They were taken to the government medical university. It was fortunate that they had carried their medical documents with them. The paramedic who had accompanied the ambulance had communicated the details of the case to the hospital casualty and the staff was prepared to receive them.

A young Japanese neurologist Yohio attended to them. Yohio went through Sushila's papers. He examined Sushila thoroughly. He then discussed something with his senior colleague. Yohio was very efficient and competent. He also had the oriental courtesy that was making Singapore a popular destination for medical tourism for those in the west. Yohio added on another medicine to the one Sushila was already taking. She could fly home the next day as planned. Yohio warned her that she might feel a little dopey with the new drug.

Yohio's boss Tano knew of the epilepsy center where Sushila had undergone her surgery and was a friend of Ramesh, the surgeon who had operated on her. He was highly appreciative of their work. He gave Sujatha a note for Sushila's surgeon.

Sushila and her family reached back without further incident. They went for a review at the epilepsy centre. An MRI scan and an EEG were repeated. The scan was normal. There was some slowing of the EEG in some leads, but no definite seizure pattern. The family was reassured. An odd fit might have been triggered off by a combination of excitement and sleep deprivation. A couple of doses of medicine had also been missed. Sushila could lead a normal life. She should however desist from driving, swimming and climbing heights. The new medicine that Yohio had given could be stopped in two weeks. The other drug would continue.

Classes started again. Sushila was now in her eleventh and Kumkum in her ninth class. Sushila was made the school captain and Kumkum received a special prize for her academic achievements. Ram's daughters were the toast of the teachers and the envy of other parents. Sushila was now attending a coaching class to prepare her for the medical entrance examinations. With school classes, extra curricular affairs and coaching classes, hers days were full. The next year was even tougher. Both the sisters were preparing for their board examinations. The lights in their study room was rarely out before the early hours of the morning.

It is no easy matter to get selected to one of the medical colleges in India. The majority of these colleges are owned by the government. Entrance to these colleges is based on the results of a multiple choice entrance examination. This common entrance test is held with examination centers all over the country soon after the twelfth boards. The questions asked are based on the 12th school syllabus. There are specialized centers all over the country training children for this test. With all this intensive coaching, often starting well before their tenth class, a good number of children could score near perfect scores in this test. A lot depended on how alert you were on that particular day.

A few national institutes conducted their own entrance tests. To write these tests, you had go to these centers. You had to go to a strange city and stay in some hotel room. Rail reservations were difficult to get and flight bookings expensive. There were private medical colleges too. Many of these institutions were substandard and survived only on the capitation fees they received from students. The odd private institution which maintained high standards demanded donations that put them were well beyond the reach of the salaried class.

After the 12th examination, the countdown to the entrance examinations started. Sushila scored good grades in her twelfth board. Her grades in the common entrance examination were average. She could possibly get selection into one the government colleges in a remote location. Going to a second rate medical college in a strange place was not worth it. She would have to stay in some dingy hostel. Being a girl was a major disadvantage. One could not be sure one's safety in many places in north India. After the results started trickling in, realization settled in. If she wanted to join a medical college, she would have to waste a year, prepare afresh and try again. Sushila was pragmatic. She decided that dental and vetinary colleges were not her cup of tea. There was a reputed college at Kochi, which offered a graduation course in biotechnology. If she joined there, she could be home at least for weekends.

Sushila was disappointed. She was interested in doing research in human genetics. She would never be actually treating patients, but maybe she could get at the root cause of some diseases. Kumkum had topped the school in her tenth and joined the mathematics stream for her eleventh.

Sujatha's mother had been diagnosed to have breast cancer. Her breast was removed and she was now receiving radiation and chemotherapy at a private hospital. The tumor had not been an aggressive one. Unfortunately she had not told any one about the lump in her breast. It was only after her attempts to pray away the lump had failed that she had agreed to visit the hospital. The oncologist had examined her. There was no obvious systemic spread, but cancer cells could be hiding in her bones or lungs. Chemotherapy could knock out some, but not all of these cells.

Cancer treatment was expensive and she had not been covered by medical insurance. Sujatha was in a bit of a spin. She had to balance looking after her mother in hospital with running home. Fortunately the girls were now grown up and responsible and they had a reliable maid who did the cooking and the cleaning.

Ramachandran would have to move to Dubai for some time. The company had a large clientele of NRI's and they had decided to set up a branch office there. The money would be good there and with two girls going into marriageable age, the cash could come in handy.

The radiation and chemotherapy courses were soon over. Her treatment course was completed. Sujatha's mother now returned home. There was no evidence of any residual disease, but only time would tell. She would need to go for a check up and a rescan of her chest, spine and liver after six months.

Sushila's college was due to start. She would stay at the YWCA hostel, which was close to her college. It was much neater although a bit more expensive than the college hostel. The secretary of the YWCA was related to the family and would smooth out any difficulties she might face. The college however was a disappointment for Sushila. She had been tuned to the intense preparation and was used to the burning ambition of her class fellows while preparing for the medical entrance tests. Here in college, the majority of students were laid back and seemed to be least interested in their careers. Most of the discussions were on movies and cricket. The girls seemed reconciled to early marriages. If they pursued careers after marriage, it would be out of their spouse's avarice and not of a desire to fulfill their own aspirations.

The YWCA hostel was comfortable, although it was a far cry from the pampered coziness of her home. Sushila was now slim and tall by Kerala standards and she carried herself well. She dressed simply, but in good taste. The college she studied in was conservative and jeans were considered to be bordering on the immoral. The sexual apartheid was rigidly enforced, with boys and girls sitting in separate sections in class and having separate canteens for their breaks. You could barely talk to the opposite sex without ruining your reputation. She found the college atmosphere stifling and restrictive.

Chapter 15   Sushila finds a Mentor

Ramachandran had moved to Dubai. Sujatha continued her teaching, looked after her mother and helped Kumkum with her books, whenever she needed help. Kumkum was very bright. She did her preparations without attending any of the coaching classes. She did her studying on her own and looked to her mother mainly for emotional support. The grand parents were now avid bridge players.

In the evenings Ram's parents would come over to Sujatha's place, where the two old couples sat and played bridge. Kumkum would sit in her room in her father's house and study. They had a dog there, a Labrador named Rex. Whenever she got tired of her books, she would play with Rex or take him for a walk. She missed her sister and looked forward to the weekends when she would come home.

Sujatha was now the vice principal of the school and her responsibilities had increased. She had a flair for administration and the principal would depend on her more and more whenever something important had to be done.

When Sushila came home for the weekends, she would complain to her mother about the uninspirational character of her college education. Sujatha was helpless. Ram's views on college education for girls had been molded by the ethos of the state. He looked at Sushila's college education as part of her preparation for the marriage arena. Sulatha was sure that Sushila's plans of going abroad for her education would be vetoed by him. Kumkum was of the opinion that Sushila should have another shot at the medicine entrances. It would be pointless, thought her mother. Sushila would not be able to juggle her college education and cntrance exam preparations. The logistics were insurmountable and half-hearted attempts just would not work out.

Sujatha pampered her daughter when she was at home and packed little tiffins for her snacks during the week. Sushila would have to adjust. Besides, the biotechnology related opportunities in the pharmaceutical field were poised to zoom. The Indian pharmaceutical industry was rediscovering itself and there would be plenty of job opportunities. Once she was independent and earning for herself her father would find it more difficult to come between her and any dreams she might have.

Sushila appreciated the merit of her mother's advice. She could not achieve anything by being impatient. Life was waiting for her. She would take it one step at a time. She started focusing on her college work. There was a biotechnology teacher whom she admired. The students knew her as Mrs. Eapen. Ms Eapen had worked in a genetic research lab in the United Kingdom for three years, when her husband had been posted there as a diplomat. When he retired and came back to India, she had accompanied him. There was no genetic research worth mentioning in India.

The teaching job in the college had been convenient for her. However she missed the ambience and the work ethos of the lab. "A woman always has to compromise", she would say. Sushila soon became Mrs Eapen's favorite student. She would borrow her teacher's journals and books on genetic engineering. Soon she could discuss genetic engineering intelligently with her mentor. She would stay back, the weekends when Mrs Eapen's husband was out of town. Eapen was working on a text book for the masters course and Sushila was helping her with it.

Kumkum's twelfth boards were over and she was going around the country with her mother and grandfather on the entrance examination circuit. Sujatha's mother was stable for now and would look after herself for a few days. Kumkum was confident of making it into one of the top technology institutes in the country. Her confidence in herself was justified. When the entrance examination results came out, she had been selected for the IIT. With her national rank of fifty, she could choose the institute of her choice and get her choice of majors. She chose computer science.

The celebrations over Kumkum's selection were barely over. Sujatha's mother was unwell and back in the hospital. She had developed a backache. The initial X-Rays had been reported as normal. An MRI however had shown some suspicious lesions in her spine, which could well be deposits from her breast cancer. They would start a course of radiation and chemotherapy for her again, this time focusing on the spine. She would have to remain in bed for about eight weeks till the bones healed after the tumor was knocked out with radiation.

With her mother confined to bed, Sujatha had her hands full. She continued her work at school. She had completed her management course through a distance education program and was raring to go. Sujatha had planned to move out of teaching into something more exciting after her girls were in college. With her mother bedridden however, her ambitions had to be put on hold.

Ramachandran's visits to India were fewer now. There were many young management graduates snapping at his heels. If he slackened in his work, he would be out of the reckoning. He worked late hours and was constantly under pressure. One evening he was still in his office at eight, when he received a fax message. A business school graduate who had recently joined the firm would be coming to Dubai to take charge of the entire project. Ram could continue to work under him or opt to come back to India. This was the end.

He had seen this coming for a long time. A caste system now pervaded the business world. B-school products would only talk to each other. All the others had to settle for the second rung. Some called it the B-school mafia. It was effective and ruthless. Companies soon realized that if they were to break into big time, their front men had to have a business school pedigree.

Ram wrapped up the day's work and poured himself some coffee. The others in his office had already left for home. Ram called the security officer and asked him to lock up. He had had enough. He would go back to Kerala and settle down. He fondly thought of Sujatha and his young daughters. He had been neglecting them.

He reached his flat and lay down without bothering to take off his shoes. There was a feeling of tightness in his chest. The coffee had not agreed with him. He noticed that he was sweating. The pain in his chest was increasing. Soon it felt as if his sternum was caught in a hot pincer. Ram sighed in desperation. He was knowledgeable enough to realize that he was having a heart attack. He got up to go to the telephone to ring for help. He did not make it. He collapsed in a heap midway between the bed and the telephone table. They found his body the next morning. The flat cleaner sensed that something was wrong when there was no response to the doorbell. They flew the body down to Kerala.

Chapter 17   Sushila's Plans

Kumkum had flown down from Bombay. Ram's sister Rekha had flown down from the United States with her son. Deepak had finished his schooling from the US. The mother wanted to use this visit to get him admitted into a private medical college. Ram's father paid the capitation fees.

There was a week of sorrowful stocktaking after Ram's final rites were over. The family was well off and the daughters were on track for successful careers. Sujatha brushed aside the suggestion that they get Sushila married. Sushila had been quite horrified at the thought. There was so much she wanted to do in life. It was her life and she had the right to choose what she wanted with it. She would soon be completing her graduation. The girls went back to their colleges. Sujatha rejoined her school again. The principal was retiring that year and she had been offered the post.

Their cousin Deepak had joined a medical college at Bangalore. Rekha was now staying with her parents in their house. Sujatha found her to be manipulative, greedy and mean. Yet she knew that she had to maintain cordial relations with her.

Sushila finished her graduation. Mrs Eapen had written to a university in the United States recommending a scholarship for Sushila. Eapen was keen that Sushila should complete her masters in genetic engineering from an apex institute. The university agreed to a fifty percent scholarship. Sushila and Mrs Eapen sat down with Sujatha to chalk out the girl's future. Sujatha was not very optimistic about sending her daughter abroad.

Ram's parents were keen on getting Sushila married off. Sujatha was certain that her sister in law was behind the whole scheme. The boy in question had finished his graduation a couple of years ago and was preparing for his chartered accountancy. Rekha insisted that this was certainly the best time to marry off Sushila.

With her history of epilepsy and brain surgery, it would be difficult enough to find her a husband. The dowry would be steep. If she went abroad for her education, most of the Kerala families would be put off. "Of what use was education to a woman, if she were not married"? Rekha would ask. Besides, the property was all still in Ramachandran's father's name. How would they finance the venture?

Sujatha's mother was dying. The disease had now appeared in her brain and lungs. Options for chemotherapy and Radiotherapy had all been exhausted. The doctors were just aiming to keep her comfortable for as long as they could before she died. There was a tube passed through her nose for feeding her. She kept needing higher and higher doses of pain killers for her back pain. When the medication wore off, she was in agony. Her cognition was intact and she sensed her end was near.

Sujatha would sit by her side into the evening. One day Sushila was also there with her and they talked about the girl's plans. Sushila had no intention of getting married now and definitely not to the kind of man her father's people had in mind. They did not have the money to send her to the United States. With Rekha influencing her parents Sushila's paternal grandparents would offer no support.

Her grandmother called her husband. There was a plot of land by the rivers edge which belonged to them. They could sell this and use the money to finance her studies. Sujatha agreed. There was one condition. Her in-laws should not know where the money was coming from. It would be told that Sushila was getting a full scholarship for a project for one year. They could keep talking about extensions after that.

As they had expected, Ram's parents were reluctant to let her go abroad. Rekha was the most vehemently opposed to the idea. Fortunately for Sushila, the boy whom they had in mind for her had failed his chartered accountancy examination. His parents wanted to let him have one more shot at it before he married. If he cleared his examination, the dowry that they could demand would be much higher. Reluctantly, the family agreed to let Susheela go for a year. After all, it was not costing them anything.

Sushila bid a tearful farewell to her dying grandmother. Her college in the US was opening in two weeks. She would have to stay with Kumkum at Mumbai to finish the necessary visa documentation and then she would be off. She knew that she would never get to see her grandmother again.

Sujatha was uncomfortable in her in laws house now. Her sister-in-law was constantly making barbed remarks about her inability to look after Ram's parents. The fact that Sujatha's mother was dying and that she was managing her school work in addition to looking after her mother seemed to be conveniently forgotten. Ram's sister had never been employable or employed. She seemed to blame Sujatha for her brother's early demise.

There was nothing that Sujatha could do to satisfy Rekha. Sujatha had to be look after her mother. School was the bastion where she could maintain her sanity and her dignity. Sujatha was smart enough to realize that her sister in law had designs on Ram's parental property. Traditionally the house and land would go to the son's family. Rekha definitely had other ideas. Sujatha only hoped that Sushila and Kumkum would never need to settle in Kerala and squabble with their aunt and cousin on property shares.

Sushila was met at the airport by Elizabeth, a girl of Indian origin who studied in the university. Liz would be her roommate for the next one year. In their second year they would both have single rooms. Liz told Sushila about the program she would attend and about the campus in general.

At least thirty percent of the students were Indians. They had Indian associations and Indian festivals. Elizabeth warned her about getting too involved in this cultural identity business. The American students were more likely to show restraint and polish with the girls than many of the Indian boys. Indians carried their masochistic attitudes with them when they came overseas. They would not dare to try funny stuff on any of the American girls. They wanted the Indian girls to be their girl friends, when they were in the university. Invariably they would go back to India for a short break, once they managed a job. They all came back with innocent Indian girls in tow who would stay at home and keep house for them while they continued their affairs. "Never get too close to any Indian boy on Campus" was Liz's advice.

The highways in the US were wider and larger than any she had ever imagined. The buildings were taller and the cars more posh. Even the people seemed bigger. "Every thing looks king sized", Sushila commented. Liz nodded. She had had the same feeling when she had first come to the states. They both laughed.

Liz showed her around campus. It was beautifully kept and spotlessly clean. There was no dirt or grime. Sushila understood why people from the west often looked down upon India. Culture and tradition were the curtains we drew over the grime and the squalor.

Chapter 19   Sushila at the University

Sushila was still on medication. She had got herself reviewed by the neurologist before leaving. He had given her three months quota of medicines. She would have to continue treatment with the university doctor after that.

Her academic programs started. It was a whole new world for Sushila. The field of genetic engineering was evolving. Sushila's interest was in human genetics. Even there, there were myriad openings. There were teams working on the unraveling of the human genome. Many groups were working on therapeutic genetics. There would soon be medications which were tailored to suit a persons genetic code. Custom tailored therapeutic regimes would be of application not only in cancers and genetic disorders but even in common systemic diseases like hypertension and diabetes.

One of the more eminent professors on campus was Professor Hamilton. Sushila had an opportunity to listen to one of his discourses. Prof Hamilton's life work had been on the role of the genome in the evolution of the species. His hypothesis on the reverse transcription of acquired characters was controversial and thought provoking. After listening to him Sushila was convinced that she wanted to pursue this aspect of research as her thesis. She would be able to opt for her guide only after her first semester was over.

Ms Eapen's tutelage was proving invaluable. She was well ahead of most of her class in her understanding of the concepts of genesis. Liz and others were impressed by her understanding of the topic and looked up to her for help and advice. Sushila scored straight A's in all her subjects. She could now knock at Hamilton's door.

The Professor tried to discourage her. What he was doing was pure research with no commercial application. Most people from India and Egypt who studied in their university were keen on doing projects which would land them well paid jobs in the industry. Sushila convinced him that money was not her motive. She was genuinely interested in what he was doing. Hamilton was pleased. He knew that Indians were often averse to accepting a black man as their guide. This girl was so different from the rest. He asked her to report to his laboratory the next morning.

The leader of the research unit was the professor's son. His name was Philip and he had one of the best academic track records in the university. Sushila reported to him. Philip showed her around the laboratory. There were so many fossils around that Sushila raised an eyebrow. Philip reassured her. The fossils were all sources of DNA. There was a gene that Hamilton believed existed. He called it the evolution gene. This was the key to the normally locked and secure genetic code. When an acquired character was to be inherited, the evolution gene had to be triggered. As of now, the evolution gene remained elusive. The skeptics claimed that it was a myth.

Sushila started her work under Philip's supervision. She was a fast learner and he could soon trust her with the gene labeling. There was a lot of patient and meticulous genetic labeling involved before they could identify the pattern of change in genetic codes with evolution. I t was hard work, searching for the elusive holy grail of genetics, the evolution trigger.

Kumkum was one of the brightest of bright sparks in her IIT batch. She was always in time with her assignments. The professors loved her. She had none of the airs and graces of the other bright girls and was down to earth in her outlook. She had been fantasizing about the institute ever since she could remember and mopped up all the information she could get like a sponge. She was a little disappointed with the attitudes of the other students. They were all incredibly bright, but they lacked commitment to any cause. There were very few with any interest in research or in the pursuit of knowledge for its own sake. They all planned to join the top management institutes after their technical courses.

After an initial phase of disillusionment, she reconciled herself. Kumkum soon understood how the system worked. The selection process to the IIT was so demanding that only the most talented would get in. This was the key. The technical education was just icing on the cake. Even if you taught these youths Indian history before sending them out into the job markets they would still make a mark. The institutes got the best of talent and than prepared them for managing a technological world. There was little room for ivory tower scholars.

Kumkum was enjoying the training despite her cynicism. She sometimes envied her friends who had joined the medical colleges. These guys were bright sparks too. But these medicos would be applying everything that they learned in their practice of medicine. "Doctors remained glorified technicians, we become technology managers", thought Kumkum with pride.

The campus life of the institute aped the social ethos of the west. Kumkum stayed clear of the dating and dances. She had so many ties to her home. She could never really let her hair down. Kumkum was aware of the politics her aunt Rekha was playing with her mother. She had no great desire for the property. It saddened her that her father's parents were being turned against her part of the family. Her maternal grandmother had finally succumbed to her cancer. Before she died she took off her gold ring and gave it to Sujatha. "Give this to Sushila" were her last words.Sujatha stayed on with her father. Rekha was downright hostile and Sujatha could not live with the constant bickering.

Kumkum remained in the mainstream of the IIT's best and the brightest. She finished her course with distinction and was selected into the Indian Institute of Management at Bangalore. She was nearer home now. Rekha had started some mumblings about the course fees. Kumkum managed to raise an educational loan for herself which covered most of her expenses. Fortunately, the banks could recognize a good investment when they saw one.

Kumkum was selected on campus as a management executive in the computer division of the Barclays international. Sujatha felt that it was time to get her married. Reluctantly Kumkum agreed. She gave her mother the go ahead to arrange her marriage. Kumkum felt that she owed her this happiness.

When Sujatha started looking around for a husband for Kumkum she was in for a shock. Kumkum's academic and professional brilliance were powerful deterrents in the marriage market. There were few boys who could come anywhere near her in academic brilliance. These men were interested in marrying rich girls who could be good hostesses or further their career prospects. The few people who showed some interest did so with the precondition that Kumkum would give up her career and stay at home.

Dilip was floundering through his medical education. The college was full of NRI children. All of them had paid upward of thirty lakh rupees to get a seat in the college. The yearly fees were steep too. It was well beyond the reach of the Indian salaried class. The affluence of the students showed in the opulence of their life styles. Many of the students zoomed around in their cars while the rest had fancy bikes. Their rooms had all the fancy electronic gadgetry possible and it was common for them to blow a few thousand rupees for a single night in town.

When Dlip came home after his first semester, he started hounding his grandparents for money for a car. Rekha tacitly supported him. Dilip's father was still in the US and showed no interest whatsoever in what his son and wife were doing. Rekha knew that her husband had a Mexican girl friend and was not concerned about his family anymore. Dilip's grandparents did not have the ready cash to buy him a car. They bought him a new powerful motorcycle. They were all however concerned when Dilip's first semester marks came in. He had failed in two out of the three subjects. Rekha rushed to her son's defence. "It was quite common for students to fail a few subjects here and there during their studies. It ultimately made them better doctors".

Dilip and his friends were living life in the fast lane. Soon it was obvious to his mother that her son would probably never clear medical school. Rekha started lying to her parents about her son's performance. She had been working on her father to change his will. The old man had bequeathed his property to Ram's family. Under Rekha's constant goading he now changed it. Rekha told him that Dilip would soon be finishing his medical education. According to her, he was planning to set up a hospital on their property in his grandfather's memory. If the property went to Ram's girls, their husbands would just sell off the property. The asset would be lost to the family forever. Dilip of course would take over the responsibility of his cousin sister's marriages. The old man fell for the tale. He amended his will. After his death, the house and property would be Dilip's.

Dilip had finished his medical course. The college would no longer let him stay on the premises. He had consistently failed his examinations and there was little possibility of his qualifying. His friends had been dabbling in business and there were good prospects if he could migrate to Canada. His mother had told him that his grandfather had changed his will in Dilip's favor. Dilip needed the capital now.

He surmised that all that stood between him and riches was his grandfather. The old coot might live for ever. By the time his granddad died, the business opportunity would be lost.

He chalked out a campaign with his friends, sitting late into the night at the 'Bulls Eye' bar. He would return to Kerala stating that he had qualified. He would get the property assessed and ready for sale without his granddad's knowledge. Then he would slowly ease the old man out of his misery. Dilip had some knowledge of pharmacology. If he applied it intelligently, the old man could be eliminated without the shadow of doubt ever falling upon him.

Sushila had heard as to how addicting research work could be. She was now experiencing it. She was spending most of time in the laboratory. She and Philip would stack a few snacks in the refrigerator. They often worked through the night. Sushila had told Philip of her seizure disorder and the surgery she had undergone. This was a good thing, because he would remind her when the medicines were due and make sure that she did not miss a dose.

The two of them had to fly down to South America for some field work Hamilton wanted them to get some DNA samples of certain monkey species which lived there. He could not believe that humans in the America's had migrated there in boats as was popularly believed. It seemed unlikely that men and women had traveled together across the Atlantic for the purpose of establishing a line of progeny. The monkeys in south America were quite different from the ones in Africa. If they had evolved independently their lineage remained an enigma. Philip and Sushila would explore the possibility and look for leads. To get an unbiased input, one had to get as near the source as possible.

In the laboratory, Philip and Sushila had been so engrossed in their work that they had not really spoken to each other about themselves. During the field trip, they had all the time in the world. Sushila told Philip about the difficulties her mother had faced to send her to the university. She told him of the warped value systems and the hypocrisy in Kerala. The caste system still pervaded the social ethos. The dowry system had been banned by law, but was perpetuated by the religious and social structure. During functions and parties, not only were men and women segregated but is still also traditional for the women to eat after the men had finished. Sushila would have to go back to India in a few years for her mother's sake.

Philips spoke of the travails his people had faced when they were brought from Africa in cargo ships. They were herded like animals and sold at auctions. There had been a long journey to emancipation. Even now there were pockets of resistance. The WASPs or white Anglo-Saxon Protestants were still a potent specter behind the scenes.

The two of them had settled into an equation of mutual trust and respect. Philip understood the social values that still bound her to her family and the values of India. Sushila looked up to Philip for guidance at every step. She cared for him deeply.

By the time they came back from the field trip they were inseparable. When his parents asked Philip whether they he and Sushila were in a relationship, he denied it. "Sushila is Indian and she needs to go back to her roots". Prof Hamilton smiled to himself. His son was one of the most eligible bachelors on campus and could pick any girl he wanted. Yet he was friendly to an Indian girl who could not enter into a relationship. The species of homo sapiens had indeed evolved.

Hamilton's hypothesis and his research work were creating major ripples in scientific circles. He was being heralded as a modern-day Darwin and the father of the genetic basis of evolution. The evolution gene he hypothesized however, still remained elusive.

Sushila wrote to her mother about Philip. She had hoped that her mother would give her some kind of a go ahead. Sujatha's reaction surprised her. If Sushila came back with a black American man, she would not be able to live in Kerala any more. Sushila's three years in the university would get over soon. Sujatha urged her daughter to come back.

When Sushila received her reply from her mother, she went to Philip. She showed him the letter and she cried. Philip knew that Sushila had to go back. "Do whatever you need to", he reassured her. "If you ever decide to come back to me, I will be waiting".

When Sushila reached Kerala, her mother was there at the airport to receive her. In the cab, on the way home she told her about all that had been happening. Dilip had come back and was busy making arrangements to construct a hospital. He had raised loans from many people in the neighborhood and taken the property deals of Ram's father's property for evaluation by consortium of builders. Once the value of the property was fully established, it would be easier to get assistance to start construction. She told her about how she had to abort Kumkum's wedding plans. Sushila smiled to herself. Kumkum and she were constantly in communication. She knew exactly what all had transpired. Kumkum was now at the Barclay's at London. She too would be coming down to India in a couple of days.

Sujatha told her daughter about the boy whom she was to marry. It was the same youth who had been proposed for her before she had left to the US. The boy whose name was Santhosh had not passed his Chartered Accountancy yet but was confident of getting through in his next attempt. He ran a financial agency now and was dabbling in stocks. Sujatha did not tell Sushila about the long negotiations on dowry which had taken place. Santhosh's people had finally agreed to the proposal. This was after Sujatha's father agreed to give away his house and property to the couple as a wedding present.

Sushila had come home determined to accept whatever her mother had planned for her. If she married a Malayalee boy, people would at the very least leave her mother and Kumkum in peace. The wedding was scheduled for a week later. Kumkum flew down from London. Sushila was a little taken aback that the boy was not even meeting her before the wedding. The whole thing was a bit sickening. She would just have to grin and bear it.

The wedding was a grand affair. A whole lot of cousins whom they had barely met had come down. One of their cousins from Bangalore was friendly to Kumkum. He had met her a couple of times at the management institute at Bangalore. He cornered her one day to ask her what Dilip was upto. He knew from his friends at Bangalore that Dilip had abandoned his medical education. There were also strong rumors that he was in the process of selling his ancestral property to a building consortium.

Here, at Kerala, everyone seemed to believe that Dilip was a doctor and that he was building a hospital It was all rather baffling. Kumkum was worried. She did not want to burden her sister with this information at her wedding. Her mother had her hands full. If she told anyone else, they would assume that she was making it up to spite Dilip for doing them out of their property share.

Sushila and Santosh shifted into Santosh's house after their wedding. Sushila had never had a need to cook and keep house before. Here she was expected to wake up early and prepare everything from the morning tea till the evening's dinner. She was spending most of the time in the kitchen.

Dilip had been working behind the scenes to sell his grandparent's house and property. He had even got the old man to sign the necessary documents. He told the man that the papers he was signing were necessary for the sanctions required to build the hospital. Ram's father was in the habit of having a couple of drinks in the evening. Ever since he came back, Dilip had been preparing his drink for him. His friends had given him a tasteless medicine that he would add to the old man's drink. The drug was a liver toxin. They had estimated that the old man's liver would fail in a month. Three months were over now. Dilip started doubling the dose of poison.

Then one night it happened. The old man cried out in his sleep, waking up his wife in the process. He was breathing heavily and then he vomited. His wife screamed, the vomitus was full of blood. Dilip and Rekha came running up. They shifted the old man to hospital. Dilip told the doctor there of his grandfather's alcohol habit. The doctor took only a minute to confirm his suspicion of liver failure. The old man's liver was huge and his abdomen was full of fluid. When he died two days later in hospital, there was not even the shadow of doubt regarding foul play. The cause of death given in the death certificate was alcoholic liver disease. The next morning the grieving widow returned home to find that her luggage had been packed in her absence by Rekha. She was being shifted to an old age home for destitute women. She tried to protest. "What about the hospital? Why would her husband sell off their house?" There was no time for answers. The taxi was waiting.

Rekha and Dilip dropped the old lady at the home, where her room was ready. A month's advance had been paid. Mother and son were on the train to Bangalore the same day. Within a week, they were in Canada.

Neither Sushila nor Sujatha had any idea of what was going on. The day after the old man's death, Sujatha had tried to ring up her mother in law. When she could not get through on the land line she had rung up Dilip on his mobile. Dilip told her that grandmother had been depressed after her husband's death. There was an old friend of her's in the old age home who was also a widow. She had gone to spend a couple of days with her. Dilip would get her back in a couple of days and then give Sujatha a call.

Two days later Sujatha's father told her that her father in law's house was being demolished. Had the hospital construction started. Where were Dilip and Rekha?

Sujatha drove over to her in-law's place. The place was being demolished. The contractor there had no inkling about any hospital plans. He had been told that a shopping mall would be coming up on the premises. Sujatha could get all the details from the office of the builder's consortium.

On a hunch she drove to the old age home. Her mother in law was there. On seeing Sujatha she burst into tears. She could not believe that her own daughter and grandson had done this to her. Sujatha packed her bags for her and brought her back to her house. Her mother in law would live with dignity as long as she was alive. The whole neighborhood was in an uproar. Many people had lost money. The loans which Dilip had taken had all been signed by his grandfather. The old man was dead and the property had been sold. There was nothing anyone could do.

Sushila was for all practical purposes, living under house arrest. Her husband would get up in the morning and leave for the stock market. In the evening he would be at the club with his friends. At night he would come home drunk and demand dinner. Some nights he never returned. He would be back in the morning, dishevelled and disorderly.

Sushila would prepare the morning tea and her husband's packed lunch. Then she would set about preparing breakfast for the rest of the family. Soon a maid would come to help with the house cleaning. Sushila often got the distinct impression that her in laws had been interested in the wedding partly to save on the maid's wages. She understood that this was how the myth of male dominance was perpetuated in Kerala society. The females were kept busy in house hold chores effectively preventing them from aspiring for achievement. "At least things could not get worse", she thought.

Sushila was wrong. Two months after the wedding she missed her period. She was pregnant. After her wedding she had suggested to her husband that they consult the neurologist on changing over to anti seizure medicines that would be safe in pregnancy. He had laughed at the idea. "Sushila had not had any seizures for years. Why was she wasting money on doctors and medicines'? He suggested that Sushila was enamored by her doctor. She was shocked by his callousness and did not bring up the topic again. She had enough stock of her old medicines.

Sushila remembered that her Neurologist had recommended an anti-epileptic drug called Lamotregene, which she switch to, when she was planning a family. On one of the rare occasions when she got to go to town, she had checked at a pharmacy. The drug was expensive. Her husband would know about it unless she was to ask her mother to buy it for her. She could not bear to tell her mother her predicament. Sushila was regretting her decision now.

The medication she was taking could have already damaged the fetus in her womb. Sushila made a decision to stop her drugs. It would, she thought, be safer for her baby. There was no respite for Sushila despite her pregnancy. She still had to do all the housework.

Sushila's husband wanted to sell her mother's house. Fortunately, the house had been gifted to both of them by her grandfather. No one could sell it as long as she did not agree. Sushila swore that she would never sell the house. Sujatha lived in it with her father and mother in law. Santosh was furious. He had lost money in the stock market and needed capital urgently. He and his parents started harassing Sushila. Sushila took all their jibes and ill treatment. She never told her mother about these developments. She knew that they would not murder her outright. Dowry deaths were something the police were on the look out for. They would never get away with it

Kumkum had come to visit, during the Christmas season. She was shocked to see her sister's status and appearance. Philip Hamilton had got in touch with her after Sushila's wedding. He asked about Sushila's welfare. Kumkum was the only person Sushila confided in. Initially Kumkum had tried to gloss over Sushila's plight with Philip. Later she started confiding in him. Sushila would suffer if anyone of her in-laws knew of Philip. Life for her was tough enough as it was. The sisters had a long talk one evening. Sushila conceded that she had made a big mistake giving up Philip and her work. Now it was too late, she was legally her husband's property.

Sushila started having minor seizures soon thereafter. She was in her sixth month of pregnancy, when she started having full blown seizures again. She had been off medicine for almost five months now. The first recurrence of a major seizure had occurred in the vegetable market, where she had gone to do her shopping. She felt the seizure coming and she had gone and sat down on a stone by the roadside waiting for the absence to pass. This time however she fell down and had a full-blown convulsive seizure. The shopkeepers had rushed her to a local hospital. She was kept there in the detention ward till late evening. Sujatha was by her side. Her husband Santosh had been informed, but he had refused to come to the hospital and take her home. Sujatha had been aware that all was not well in her daughter's house. She had not realized that things were this bad.

Sujatha took Sushila back with her to her house. The next day they visited the neurologist who had treated Sushila earlier. He was shocked to hear how she had been neglecting herself. He started her on medication again. The foetus was now reasonably mature and the medications he started would not affect it. Sushila spend almost a month with her mother. Kumkum would phone her up daily. Philip too would telephone regularly. He told her about the progress of the research work they were doing. He had been seeing Kumkum off and on and described her as "The second most fascinating woman he had ever met". Sushila smiled to herself. It had been a long time since she had smiled.

Santosh was now pressurizing her to get back to his house. He threatened to go to court. He promised to look after her well. Sujatha did not want to let her go. Sushila knew that she had to go back. She was keen that the baby should have a father. She hoped that her in-laws had changed. When Sushila went back to her in-laws, they started ill treating her again. They would not let her speak to her mother. Her mother in law confiscated her medicines. Sushila was a prisoner. Sushila was getting seizures off and on. Fortunately none of them were very severe.

Sushila was almost due for delivery. One night she started having pains. Sujatha had visited Santosh and told him that she would bear all the expenses of Sushila's confinement. There was a private hospital near their house. Santosh drove her there and went back home. He promised Sushila that he would inform her mother. He did not. Sujatha had no idea that her daughter had been admitted. Sushila's labor was not progressing satisfactorily. The hospital was not equipped for a caesarian. The doctor wanted to shift Sushila to the medical college. Santosh's mobile was switched off and he was not traceable. They dumped her in a jeep and with an Ayah in attendance, shifted her to the medical college.

Sushila started having seizures in the jeep. She was blue by the time they reached the medical college. They rushed her to the operation theatre. They passed a tube in her trachea and ventilated her. Then they operated to save the baby. It was too late. The baby was dead. Sushila was on the ventilator and in the ICU again. When Sujatha reached the hospital, the doctors were frank. Sushila had suffered severe brain damage. She might never come off the ventilator again.

Chapter 27   The End

Sujatha, Kumkum and Philip sat by Sushila's bedside. She was still on the ventilator. It was seven days now since her operation. She had defied the doctor's predictions and become conscious again. But Sushila's lungs were failing and she was not producing urine. Her blood pressure was being maintained by two drug infusions. The doctors had warned the family that she would not last the night. Near midnight they persuaded Sujatha to get some rest on the sofa.

Sushila's eyes were open. She was looking at Philip and Kumkum. She stretched her hand towards Kumkum. Holding Kumkum's hand, she placed in Philip's. A ghost of a smile seemed to flicker at the corner of her mouth. She was asking for a pen and paper. She had her ring in her hand. She scribbled, "Give this ring to your child. Name her after me". Kumkum was crying openly. Philip's eyes were moist with tears. They remained like that holding hands till the early hours of the morning. An alarm in the monitor went off at five in the morning. Sushila's heart had stopped beating.

Soon after Sushila's death Santosh sold off Sujatha's house. Sujatha shifted with her father and mother in law to Kumkum's house outside London.

A month later they flew down to the US. Kumkum and Philip were married in a quiet ceremony.

Sushil Hamilton was at school. He was showing off a gold ring on his finger to a friend in play school. "This was given for me by my Godmother, when she died. I got my name from her".

Unfinished Business

Khalil Palathinkal

It is easy to surmise, that reckoning is due

To say that we fulfilled our destiny is only partly
true

Yet hills loom ahead, their slopes forbidding

The flesh is weak and our tired legs are aching

There was a time, when the whole world was our
stage

Options were myriad, time on our side

Time ran out, options dwindled and infirmness of
age

Caught us, as we drifted carelessly with the tide

Confrontation, we knew, was of little avail

Forces urging conformation would ultimately prevail

We learned to genuflect and float with fixed plastic smiles

Unquestioning acceptance, drab platitudes dotted every mile

The forest of life was ripe for an explorer's eye

But we chose beaten paths, comforting crowds, all in line

Hierarchies, rest stations, all in a predictable profile

The path was safe, oft trodden; we could safely rest a while

There were higher hills and larger plains where men camped

Relishing the rest after a race well run

As we trudge along, they look on with wonder

Where are we headed? Won't we rest and have fun

Ambition is habit, a quest soul's fire

A candle to explore the forest some more

The mystical rainbow, a heart's musical lyre

A flash of hope, an illusion, seen never before

The business of life remains strictly ours

Supported minimally by children, wives or lovers

In death we stand alone, a dying star in twilight

Burning in a flash of energy that is eternal

The Deception

Khalil Palathinkal

Passing through the trails of life

Buffeted by chants from every side

God, country, family, global warming

I paused to listen, but kept walking

Hollow laughter, around me rings

False promises, barbed tethers clothed in satin

Shrouds blinding, deceptions smarting

Thorns, sharpened knifes on every side

Is there truth any where, my heart aches

For the comfort, solace of a true embrace

For a glimpse of true purity, enlightenment

An end to the futility of fraudulent existence

Is there a charm, a wall, a divide

Betwixt the chaste purity of a nun in habit

And the murderous malevolence of a gun toting
Jehadi

Or are they variations of a paradigm of purity

Is the earth warming, or is that too a farce

Fostered upon a nervous populace so fettered

Fed capsules of untruth in sub lethal doses

Numbed acceptance of authority, a pervasive force

A tweet of a voice I heard from within

It was the murmur of my heart, my conscience, my
soul

God, truth and solace therein resided

My quest was over, I had reached my goal.

Life and Death

Khalil Isaac Mathai Palathinkal

The politics of harassment and intimidation

Curbing aspirations to settle old scores

Organizations deprived of the fragrance of free thought

Where sycophants rein supreme, conformists rule

Success is virtue, the success secured by networks

Mediocrity panders itself, vitiates every norm

The isolation of neglected artists being forth

Creations the organizations could never conceive

The reigns of power are at the decree

Of ogres, with contradictory goals

Can any organization ever be free

Of such delinquent, self opinionated moles

It is better, often, not to confirm

Success breeds the dishonorable sale of ones soul

To struggle alone, meet loneliness head on

To aspire for the intangible, groping for a guiding
heavenly hand

> The gift to raise oneself above the clamor
>
> Where loud varies prevail and bullies rule
>
> Loneliness is a fantasy, warm is the
> camaraderie
>
> Of dead souls, eloquent forests, the intricatee
>
> intimate fabric of infinity

Yet the dishonesty of purpose is at times so
appalling

That one seeks the camaraderie of kindred souls

As we cling to the flotsam in raging emotional seas

Will sharks chomp me or the killing cold freeze my
bones

Is there a logical end to it all

Death the great arbitrar, is he a cheat

Is there a vision of a life beyond

Do we live on in memories that crumble to
dust in the

****

9 798896 109297